KESSEL RUN

THE DIGITAL BATTLEFIELD

by

CHRIS KNOWLES

Chris Knowles

Kessel Run

Chris Knowles

Kessel Run

ALSO BY CHRIS KNOWLES

Murder in Martha's Vineyard Lodge: A Masonic Allegory

Murder in Sugarbush Lodge: A Study in Brotherhood

Murder in Georgetown Lodge: Prelude to Armageddon

A Matter of Perception

The Cambridge Incident

The Head of the Snake: The ISIS Assault on Martha's Vineyard

An Ill Wind from the East

Upon This Rock

War at the Top of the World: The Battle for the Arctic Shelf

*The Disciples in Times Square:
The ISIS Showdown at the Crossroads of the World*

The Falklands Gambit

*The Eagle, The Bear and The Dragon:
The Zumwalt's Final Trial*

The Strait of Gibraltar

Shadow Government

Patriots on the Watchtower: The Second American Revolution

Chris Knowles

Foreword

"You've never heard of the *Millennium Falcon*? It's the ship that made the Kessel run in less than 12 parsecs."

Han Solo

Star Wars: A New Hope

"It was this running joke that we were going to smuggle this new software development capability into the Air Force in 12 parsecs or less."

Bryon Kroger, Captain, United States Air Force
Chief Operating Officer
Kessel Run Experimentation Lab

Chris Knowles

Chapter One

In recent years, the evolution of Project Kessel Run, a creation of the United States Air Force and the Defense Innovation Unit Experimental (DIUx) in collaboration with Pivotal Labs and TDMK Digital of Palo Alto, California and Chantilly, Virginia respectively, was born out of the necessity to conduct airborne warfare in a more timely and efficient manner on today's digital battlefield. Its first output was a piece of software called JIGSAW which was distributed over the Department of Defense's classified network to the warfighters in the field at Air Operations Centers (AOCs) across the globe. And it revolutionized a procedure which heretofore had taken a half a day each day and reduced it to a task of no more than two to three hours.

While on a tour of Air Force installations in the Middle East in October of 2016, a delegation of consultants visited the AOC at Qatar's Al Udeid Air Base. Among them was Eric Schmidt, the Executive Chairman of Alphabet, Inc., the parent company of Google, who was serving as the Chairman of the Defense Innovation Board (DIB). The DIB's mandate was to provide the Secretary of Defense (Sec Def) with "independent advice and recommendations on innovative means to address future challenges."

Air strikes on the terrorist forces of the Islamic State in Syria (ISIS) were coordinated from Al Udeid. On their runways were some of the most sophisticated fighters and bombers in the world capable of carrying weaponry of unimaginable capabilities and proportions. But Eric Schmidt was dumbfounded by the methodology being employed to plan the Air Force's daily missions.

Throughout the AOC he saw numerous whiteboards covered in magnets and color-coded plastic 3×5 cards. When Schmidt asked the AOC commander what his biggest concern was, he was told, "I don't want them to erase my whiteboard." At Al Udeid, where the Air Force's Central Command (AFCENT) oversees operations in over 20 countries from Kazakhstan to Egypt, missions were being planned on whiteboards in concert with 43 disparate software applications which were unable to talk to one another. Among the multitude of tasks required to undertake a single operation, one of the mission-critical ones was air refueling operations.

The AFCENT Chief of Staff, Colonel Mike Drowley, told Schmidt, "We got the missions for the day, figured out what targets needed to be hit, and how much fuel was needed, who needed the fuel, and when they needed it. It was an eight- or nine-hour process [for three or more people] to try and figure all the ins and outs. It was like a Tetris game of blocks and pucks."

Schmidt told *Fast Company,* "They would actually use physical distance on the whiteboard to determine whether they could meet their mission." A person known as "the Gonker" would enter data into an Excel spreadsheet known as "the Gonkulator", while "the Planner" arranged magnetic pucks and plastic laminated cards on the whiteboard to indicate how long planes could stay in the air.

"That would generate an input that had to be manually typed in." The typist was "the Thumper", and the destination for that data was the Master Air Attack Planning Toolkit which generated an Air Tasking Order at AFCENT headquarters at Shaw Air Force Base in South Carolina. Schmidt asked Drowley if the AOC didn't have access to more modern software. His answer; "Yes, but it doesn't work."

Schmidt had been accompanied by Richard Murray, a Cal Tech professor. His comment was, " . . . this just isn't that hard a problem to solve." When he asked if you couldn't just recode the software, the response was "No". "That can't be the right answer," said Murray. But it was.

DoD regulations required that AOC software go out for competitive bids. Major General Sarah Zabel, the Air Force's Director of Information Technology Acquisition Process Development at the Pentagon, said, "It's one thing to say you're going to do business differently." But the military put out software to bid using the same acquisition processes that it uses to acquire warships, fighter aircraft, and tanks. That explained why the AOC software had remained essentially unchanged since the 1990s.

Another member of the contingent touring Al Udeid was Raj Shah who, at that time, was the managing partner of DIUx. He was also a former fighter pilot who had flown combat missions out of Iraq. "Having refueled four times a day when I was deployed, I was very familiar with the output" of the tanker planning process, he said. "I'd been in situations where the tanker didn't show for a time and, as a receiver getting gas, if they're not there you get very angry." Since the whiteboard planning process was imperfect, the Air Force was required to keep numerous KC-135 *Stratotankers* fully loaded with fuel and ready to scramble at a moment's notice.

This visit was the first call to action in a process which led, less than six months later, to the implementation of a new software program, JIGSAW, which saved hours every day and millions of dollars every week. JIGSAW cost $2.2 million. The new software saves time and is more reliable. AFCENT now scrambles two to three fewer tankers each day which cost about $250,000 per tanker. Thus, the project paid for itself in under a week. Other AOC software was rewritten by Air Force engineers working with Pivotal Software to perform the task in a matter of months where a $745 million contract with a high-profile defense contractor had yielded nothing in over five years.

The previous two years of experience in the

acquisition of software programs enabling the Air Force to reach operational preparedness to conduct combat sorties exposed the fundamental weakness in the process. From the time an acquisition officer let bids for a new piece of software until it was distributed over the classified network to the operations planning desks at the numerous combat commands could take from five to seven years. Consequently, a new, more goal-oriented and streamlined approach to program writing and implementation had been envisioned and rolled out. It utilized an emphasis on the needs, knowledge, and experience of senior airmen and the industry-standard best practices and state-of-the-art technology used by the best and the brightest in the software development community. Its name was Kessel Run.

Everything about the project was designed for speed and the ability to change direction on a dime if need be. Pivotal Labs, which partnered with the Air Force, had facilities in Silicon Valley, Boston, and Chicago. It was decided to locate Kessel Run in Boston because of its access to corporate resources as well as the gold mine of talent in its vast academic community. In order to remain flexible, instead of housing Kessel Run in Pivotal's corporate offices, they leased space from WeWork, a company with properties used to accommodate new entrepreneurships and startups with high turnover rates and the need for flexible floorplans. It managed over 10,000,000 square feet of office space spread out over 280 locations in 77 cities in 23 countries. It specialized in providing space for high tech startups which is what Kessel Run essentially was.

The project ended up taking space in an office building on Portland Street in downtown Boston large enough to initially house a staff of 90 coders and engineers from both the Air Force and Pivotal with the goal of growing its staff to 300 by the Spring of 2019. The location was only three blocks from the Boston subway system's North Station and near its infamous North End, home to the city's largest Italian enclave with its innumerable, incomparable Italian restaurants, bistros, and bakeries. It was a techie's dream and offered the opportunity, if necessary, of moving to a new location at a moment's notice should the need arise.

By 2018, Kessel Run had pushed out five air operations center applications with eight more in development. After JIGSAW had been completed, work was undertaken on two new applications which would assist in aggregating targeting information, determining the most effective method of attack to be used and the best time to attack those targets, and disseminating that information to the pilots in their pre-flight briefings. The two applications were code-named RAVEN and CHAINSAW. One was in operation by late 2017 and the other shortly thereafter.

The corporate culture of Kessel Run was more akin to Microsoft or Google than the Air Force Officer Training School or the National War College. At the office on Portland Street in Boston, a few dozen Air Force enlisted men and women worked side by side with their counterparts from Pivotal. Instead of dress blues or flight suits, the Air Force staff assigned to Kessel Run wore t-shirts, jeans, and sneakers. A handful of the airmen wore t-shirts bearing an image of their outfit's logo, the *Millennium Falcon*. Others wore t-shirts with Kessel Run's twitter account designation, "#agileAF". The "AF" stood for Air Force.

The small, open-space work area was populated by numerous keyboards and monitors spread throughout. Moving freely about were airmen, "Pivots", and consultants, congregating as need be when a particular program or application required their combined attention and expertise. This seeming lack of structure facilitated the exact kind of spontaneous collaboration which Kessel Run's projects needed to think outside the box and move the coding process along at heretofore unthought-of speed within the military.

Back at Al Udeid years earlier, Shah had turned to Colonel Oti, then head of Air Force programs at DIUx, and commented, "Why don't you guys just build this tanker whiteboard? We'll put a million bucks of DIUx money into it, but just go do this. Start tomorrow." Oti had done just that. As he was to later relate, "I literally sent out a bunch of emails to all the squadron commanders I knew out there, saying, 'Hey, does anybody have any airmen that can write code?'" Within a week he had dozens of responses. "I figured, I'll grab six guys and I'll see what they can do."

Oti had to get the plan cleared by Commander Harrigan at AFCENT. As Harrigan recalled, "I had to accept the fact that we were going to try something a bit different while we were fighting a war. I had to be willing to buy some risk." That risk paid off.

Partnering with Pivotal, four Air Force coders were paired with four Pivots in conformance with the company's adoption of a software development methodology known as "Extreme Programming". In referring to JIGSAW, Oti said, "Four months from start to in production, in use in combat operations." According to Hunter Price, Director of Air Force programs at the Defense Digital Service, in referring to the rapid shift in the acquisition process, "It was bumpy for a while. The program office went through a conversion process. They knew they were out in the wilderness, they knew the AOC wasn't working well. There was some soul searching."

Keith Salisbury, Pivotal's VP for government contracts, said, "We don't want to be anybody's outsource app development organization forever. We want our clients to understand what we do and how we do it, and most importantly, why we do it. We don't want to teach them to fish. We want to teach them to be fishing guides." Speaking of the Kessel Run Experimentation Lab, Colonel Oti had said, "By the end of this year (meaning 2019) I hope we're going to be up to 15 to 18 [applications per year]. We're out to tackle the whole AOC."

Chapter Two

In the final analysis, military supremacy of the world in the 21st century is determined by the superior technology of the weapons and delivery systems which a nation may deploy in combination with the agility with which those forces are able to improvise, adapt, and overcome changes in the environment on the field of battle. The armies of ISIS, Syria, or the Taliban in Afghanistan and Pakistan may be problematic. Nonetheless, the only two nations which are capable of fielding weaponry which is comparable to or competitive with that of the United States are the People's Republic of China and the Russian Federation.

But China and Russia each pursue totally different avenues to reach and maintain that competitiveness. For China, the route is imitation. In order to accomplish this, they use two principal methods. The first consists of simple theft. For example, an agent working on behalf of the Chinese government will attempt to obtain a position working for a contractor of the United States government which builds a military aircraft, missile, or weapon. Over time they will negotiate the contractor's human resources maze until they are in a position to have access to the blueprints for that piece of technology. They may either send them as an attachment to an email to a generic personal account which only they may open or simply smuggle them out of the secure office. The plans are then forwarded to a

Chinese government representative in either the United States or China.

Alternatively, if the agent cannot obtain a high enough government clearance to personally access the blueprints they will either identify a disgruntled employee with the necessary clearance who has expressed a desire to "get even" with their employer or simply bribe an employee who has demonstrated that their income is insufficient to meet their financial needs or desires. Then that employee will steal the plans and turn them over to the Chinese agent in return for a previously agreed upon sum of money. Should they have second thoughts, their liability in a clear case of espionage which would land them in a federal prison for an extended period of time serves as a deterrent from exposing the agent. Chinese nationals or those working on their behalf have already been arrested, prosecuted, found guilty, and sent to prison for just such crimes.

The second means of obtaining those same blueprints is hacking. The People's Liberation Army (PLA) of China has set up an entire operation, Unit 61398, in an office building in Shanghai whose sole mission is to hack into other nations' government computers or those of their contractors. In the United States, those targeted could be the State Department or the Department of Defense. But they might just as easily be Raytheon or Lockheed Martin. In the case of State, the goal may be gaining access to diplomatic correspondence with American allies while at DoD the target might well be tentative Orders of Battle.

As for Raytheon, their computers could lead to the blueprints of the next iteration of a ballistic missile while the computers at Lockheed Martin could hold the plans for the next generation of stealth fighter or bomber. Should anyone question whether such activity actually takes place, they need only look to the skies at the annual China International Aviation and Aerospace Exhibition in Zhuhai in Guangdong province, 35 miles West of Hong Kong.

The People's Liberation Army Air Force's (PLAAF) latest warplane, the new J-20 fifth-generation stealth fighter (officially named *Weilong* or "powerful dragon"), is one of the world's most advanced fighter jets and is essentially a clone of the American F-22 *Raptor*. The two are virtually identical in length, wingspan, and weight. They have similar operational ceilings and can both fly at speeds in excess of Mach 2. Finally, they both carry their payloads internally in bomb bays which enhances their stealthiness over aircraft which carry their missiles externally on hardpoints attached to their wings or fuselage

Additionally, China's PLAAF has built its new J-31 *Shenyang*, or "falcon hawk", joint strike fighter to compete with the American F-35 *Lightning II*. As with the J-20 vs. F-22 comparison, both aircraft have similar lengths, wingspans, and weights. Their combat radii are within 43 nautical miles of one another. The most striking difference is that while the F-35 is a single-jet aircraft, the J-31 is propelled by twin jet engines. The F-35 flies at Mach 1.6 while the J-31 can reach Mach 1.8. The J-31 even looks and flies like the F-35.

Russia has adopted a totally different means of staying competitive in the skies over contested territory. Two of its four workhorse warplanes' airframes, that is aircraft bodies and silhouettes, date back to the early 1970s, one to the mid-1980s, and the newest to 2010. Rather than spending excessive time working on new, more aerodynamic airframes, since Russian and Soviet rocket scientist Konstantin Tsiolkovsky all but invented the wind tunnel technology of designing fuselages with minimum drag as far back as 1897, they focused on designing new engines, new avionics, new electronic countermeasures (ECMs), and new weaponry.

Both China and Russia have recently announced *and* displayed their latest military technological developments. During the last days of December 2018, hazy images of a Chinese warship with a strangely-shaped large gun mounted on its bow began circulating, first in intelligence circles and shortly thereafter in the press. It turned out to be the world's first railgun mounted on a naval vessel and now ostensibly operational. Subsequently, an image of an ungainly ship bearing an oversized gun on a blue water mission appeared on China's tightly controlled social media networks. It was significant if only because the U.S. Navy had been at work on a railgun of its own for a quarter of a century.

In 2015, the China Aerospace & Industry Corporation announced, "Railguns use electromagnetic energy to attack targets and are considered an advanced technology that offers greater range and more lethality, while the cost is even cheaper than traditional guns." The speed and range are achieved by generating an electromagnetic field between two rails. A conductive sling called an armature catapults a warhead between the rails. The projectile is traveling at a speed of 5,816 miles per hour, or Mach 7.6, when it leaves the barrel and has been shown to be able to hit a target 125 miles away in 90 seconds.

The stress of acceleration, speed, and friction is such that totally new alloys and designs have had to be developed to accommodate them. While the projectiles can be "dumb" missiles like cannonballs, they can also be fitted with explosive warheads and both avionics and sensors to help them find their target. It is estimated that each projectile will cost in the range of $75,000, far less than a guided missile.

The Type 072II *Yuting* class tank landing ship *Haiyangshan* was converted to become an experimental testbed. While not a conventional warship like a guided missile cruiser, the *Haiyangshan* can carry an extensive array of batteries and generators in its open cargo bay to power the next-generation weapon. And unlike the use of conventional projectiles or guided missiles, it eliminates the heat, pressure, and residue of gunpowder-powered cannons or either solid- or liquid-propelled missiles.

In February 2018, the *People's Daily Online* stated, "Though the test rail gun is not the final version of the high-tech weapon, its size does fit the 055 destroyer, which would become an invincible vessel once equipped with electromagnetic weapons."

Thus it appears that projectiles traveling at hypersonic speeds are the latest development in the arms race. Ironically, on December 26th, just three days earlier, the Kremlin reported that Russia had test-launched the *Avangard* hypersonic glide vehicle which flies 27 times faster than the speed of sound and is capable of carrying megaton-class nuclear weapons. The "vehicle" was called by Russian President Vladimir Putin a "New Year's present to the nation."

The *Avangard* was launched from Dombarovskiy missile base in the southern Ural Mountains and successfully hit a practice target on the Kamchatka peninsula, 3,700 miles away. Although the glider, carrying nuclear weapons, was unveiled alongside the RS-28 SARMAT "nuke-carrying" intercontinental ballistic missile, super-fast drone torpedoes, cruise missiles with nuclear power plants, the Kinzhal nuclear-capable air-launched ballistic missile system, and laser and hypersonic weapons, the German newspaper *Die Welt* characterized it as so much saber-rattling in light of the election of the new populist American President John Jefferson.

As former Russian Defense Minister Sergei Ivanov revealed, the truly threatening aspect of the *Avangard* is its maneuverability, constantly changing course and altitude while flying through the atmosphere, zigzagging its way to its target, making it impossible to predict weapon's location *or* the location of the weapon's target. This ensures that the hypersonic missile's target remains unknown until it reaches it, concluded analysts at the RAND (a contraction of Research ANd Development) Corporation.

General John Hyten, Commander of the U.S. Strategic Command (STRATCOM), has said, "We have no defense that could prevent the use of such a weapon against us." Michael Griffin, ex-chief of NASA, told an expert panel contemplating radar detection of the *Avangard*, "You have to cover thousands of miles, not hundreds," pointing out the curvature of the Earth which limits the coverage of radars, taking into account the vastness of the western Pacific Ocean and the lack of islands upon which to place the requisite radar installations. "There are not many places where radars can be parked," he said. "And if you find them, they'll probably become targets."

The best solution would be to install a network of reconnaissance sensors in space. Griffin added that not only

Russia but China were working intensively on hypersonic weapons which surpassed the United States current state-of-the-art technology to either detect or intercept them. "China tested more hypersonic weapons last year than we did in a decade. We have to change that," he stated. Faced with these developments, the Defense Advanced Research Projects Agency (DARPA) issued an urgent call for papers under the heading "Glide Breaker Program" on November 6th, 2018. Although the exact contents of the request remain classified, it is known that the call was for proposals for systems which could detect and defend against hypersonic weapon gliders in the upper layers of the atmosphere.

Chapter Three

Much of the *tactical* advantage which Project Kessel Run provided the United States lay in its agility to respond to, or prepare for, military encounters with a minimum of lead time. Should an adversary unexpectedly attack an ally or otherwise friendly nation, Kessel Run could role play innumerable iterations of potential scenarios to settle upon the actions the American forces should take to result in the most advantageous outcome. By the same token, if the National Command Authority should issue orders to take offensive action against a foe anywhere in the world, Kessel Run could not only test out various plans of attack, but it could issue orders in a matter of hours, rather than days or months, to ensure that the needed hardware, software, and troops were in the right place at the right time to see that the attacks could be carried out as directed.

Logistics is a time-consuming, laborious, and boring task. But Kessel Run was capable of determining the most efficient means of routing aircraft, warships, tanks, and troops to the location where they would be needed when the hostilities began. Moreover, it could ensure that bullets, missiles, rockets, and bombs were pre-positioned where needed when the forces undertook their missions.

As demonstrated, the United States would have to be smarter and faster at both issuing and executing orders given than their most likely adversaries, China or Russia. The question which had been posed by Peter Singer, a strategist and Senior Fellow at New America, was, "It's basically, are they producing weapon systems that have fifth-generation characteristics that potentially nullify some of our planned advantages in the future battlespace? We were depending more so on the [American weapons] having that generation-ahead edge, and if we don't have that generation-ahead edge [anymore], that is incredibly scary for us in various scenarios."

Defense Secretary Robert Work and acquisition chief Frank Kendall had been telling both the Jefferson Administration and Congress since 2016 that the U.S. military's technology advantage was eroding. Kendall had said of Russia and China's cyberespionage, "What it does is reduce the cost and lead time of our adversaries to doing their own designs, so it gives away a substantial advantage." That meant the American military would have to work both smarter and faster. That's where Kessel Run came in.

Cyberespionage allowed America's enemies to get access to the methods and tactics developed over years of planning "for the cost of breaching your network," Singer had said. Cybertheft had allowed China to save tens of billions of dollars in research-and-development, the experimentation and testing a new weapon goes through before it reaches the battlefield. Although the Chinese jet fighters may have been nominally inferior to their American prototypes since they had not had to do the early research and development it allowed them to focus upon upgrades and improvements. The 10- to 20-year advantage which the United States had believed they had over their enemies had disappeared. "Those future competitions will be incredibly difficult because we'll have paid the R&D for our competitors."

Those increased R&D costs frequently led to a decrease in the number of units purchased. In the case of the Navy's *Zumwalt* class destroyers, the R&D costs had caused the number to be purchased to be decreased from 32 to three. As for the F-22 *Raptor*, the Air Force had originally wanted in excess of 700 aircraft. That number was first cut to 381 and ultimately to 187. "The expense of our fifth-generation [fighter aircraft] means we have not been able to buy as many as we want," said Singer.

He pointed out that while the Chinese planes might still have had inferior systems, stealing intellectual property and the subsequent R&D savings had allowed Beijing to make drastic changes in the prototypes. As for the J-20, the Chinese stealth fighter built using stolen intellectual property developed for the American F-22, Singer stated that there had been numerous prototypes in which the plane's design had become stealthier. "Their designs, their capabilities are shifting from prototype to prototype in a way that has not been happening with the current way that we are building our fifth-gen systems," he said.

Whatever the reason, American planners and forces would have to become more efficient. Additionally, they would have to be able to adapt to their adversary's moves at the drop of a hat. Unlike Vietnam, Iraq, Afghanistan, or Syria, they would not have the luxury of time, nor its inherent drawback of vulnerability, to overthink it. If they took it, the enemy would be upon them in an instant.

The leadership at the Pentagon, backed up by numerous studies conducted by military think tanks, had revealed that the three most likely venues where an armed conflict could occur between the United States and one of its two principal adversaries, China or Russia, were the South China Sea, Syria, or Ukraine. As for the South China Sea, military encounters had taken place before, but they had never led to a shooting war. The entire provocation was a function of China's manufacturing man-made islands in the midst of the Paracel and Spratly archipelagoes.

These islands had been constructed by beginning with a reef or atoll, bringing in seagoing dredging equipment to suck sand up from the ocean floor to fill them in, and then constructing offices and barracks, airfields and hangars, and installing aircraft, warships, and artillery. The goal was two-fold. First, they could claim territorial waters around these islands and an ADIZ (Air Defense Identification Zone) above them to limit access by enemy warships and aircraft. Secondly, they could use these bases of operation to control or hijack the flow of both crude oil and liquefied natural gas passing through the shipping lanes of the South China Sea.

It was estimated that during the '80s, at least 270 oil and natural gas tankers had used the routes each day. Currently, more than half the world's crude oil transported by tanker passes through the South China Sea, a figure rising steadily with the growth of the PRC's consumption of oil. This figure is more than three times that passing through the Suez Canal and five times more than the Panama Canal.

Moreover, the four largest importers of liquefied natural gas (LNG) which passes through the South China Sea are Japan, South Korea, China, and Taiwan, collectively accounting for 94% of the sea lane's total volume. Japan is the world's largest LNG importer, and slightly more than half of all of Japan's LNG imports are shipped by way of the South China Sea. Similarly, about two-thirds of the LNG imported by South Korea – the world's second-largest LNG importer – is shipped through the South China Sea. More than two-thirds of China's LNG imports and more than 90% of Taiwan's LNG imports pass through the South China Sea. Total imports of LNG to China have more than doubled, increasing from 0.56 trillion cubic feet (Tcf) to 1.20 Tcf.

As for the potential of armed conflict in Syria, the encounters would most likely be with the air forces of Russia, one of only two close allies with Syria, the other being Iran. The ongoing conflict in Syria is widely viewed as a series of overlapping proxy wars between the regional and world powers, primarily between the U.S. and Russia, and secondarily between Iran and Saudi Arabia. Since 2015, Russia, the only foreign power that has its military assets openly and legally positioned in Syria, has ostensibly waged an intense air war against ISIS, although it has appeared to many, including the United States, that the primary target of the air offensive has been the Syrian rebels fighting against the oppressive regime of President Bashar al-Assad.

The Syrian rebel forces receive financial, logistical, political, and military support from major Sunni states in the Middle East who are friendly with the United States, most notably Saudi Arabia, Qatar, and Turkey. In addition, major Western European countries such as France and the United Kingdom have provided political, military, and logistical support to those rebel forces not deemed terrorists.

Russia has been a military ally of Syria since 1956, and during the Syrian Civil War it supplied Assad's regime with arms, sending military and technical advisers to train Syrian soldiers to use the Russian-made weapons as well as repairing and maintaining Syrian weapons. Some reports have suggested that Russia is helping to keep the Syrian economy afloat by surreptitiously transporting hundreds of tons of banknotes into the country by military aircraft. It has also been reported that Russian military personnel, under the cover of military advisers, were operating some of the anti-aircraft defenses provided Syria by Russia.

The potency of Syria's air defenses was a major factor in the United States' decision not to intervene in the conflict with military aircraft or impose a no-fly zone should the Assad government choose to use chemical weapons against their own citizens, which they did. Russian and American representatives met at the United Nations at the General Assembly in 2015. The subject of the negotiations was the West's continued criticism of Russia's support for the Assad government. Russia pointed out that its actions did not violate international law and Russian President Putin stated that his country did not support "any side [in the conflict] from which the threat of a civil war may emerge."

In December 2013, Russia was reported to have stepped up its military support for the Syrian government by supplying new armored vehicles, surveillance equipment, radars, electronic warfare systems, spare parts for helicopters, and various weapons including guided bombs for its aircraft. In September 2015, with permission of the upper house of the Russian Parliament, Russia started a direct military intervention in Syria consisting of air strikes against the Syrian rebels, ISIS, and other enemies of the Syrian government. The Russian Orthodox Church characterized the Russian military intervention in Syria as a "holy fight" against terrorism.

In the Fall of 2015, the U.S. ruled out military cooperation with Russia in Syria. However, on October 20th,

2015, the U.S. and Russia signed a secret technical memorandum of understanding to avoid air incidents over Syria. Nonetheless, on November 22nd Bashar al-Assad said that within two months of its air strikes on ISIS Russia had achieved more than the U.S.-led coalition had accomplished in a year.

At the end of December 2015, senior U.S. officials internally acknowledged that Russia had achieved its central goal of stabilizing the Assad government and, with the costs and casualties relatively low, was in a position to sustain the operation at this level for years to come. This did mean, however, that both American and Russian aircraft ran the risk of entering the same airspace and because of the increased tension between these two of the world's three superpowers the potential for armed conflict still existed.

Finally, there was Ukraine. It posed the greatest potential for a shooting war.

Chapter Four

In a military offensive staged by a joint force of
embedded rebel Russian loyalists and the Russian military,
the Crimean peninsula, which juts out into the Black Sea
from the Southeastern coastline of Ukraine, was seized by
Russia in an operation which took place in February and
March of 2014. Since that time, Crimea has been
administered by the Russian Federation as two subjects, the
Republic of Crimea and federal city of Sevastopol, its
capital. The seizure was accomplished by Russian military
intervention in Crimea following the 2014 Ukrainian
revolution and the more widespread unrest in Southern and
Eastern Ukraine.

On the night spanning the 22nd and 23rd of February,
2014, Russian President Vladimir Putin conducted a meeting
with his security service leaders. At the conclusion of the
meeting, Putin is reported to have said, "[W]e must start
working on returning Crimea to Russia." That day, pro-
Russian demonstrations were held in the Crimean capital
city of Sevastopol and on the 27th Russian troops wearing
army uniforms with no identifying insignia captured the
Supreme Council, or parliament, of Crimea as well as
strategic sites across the province. On March 16th, Crimea
conducted a status referendum and declared Crimea's
independence from Ukraine. Two days later, Russia
incorporated Crimea as part of the federation.

Locally and around the world, Ukrainian and national leaders condemned Crimea's annexation and deemed it a violation of both international law and agreements signed by Russia ensuring Ukraine's territorial integrity. The G-8, a political forum of the world's leading industrial nations, suspended Russia's membership and the UN General Assembly rejected the vote and annexation, adopting a non-binding resolution affirming the "territorial integrity of Ukraine within its internationally recognized borders." It went on to underscore "that the referendum having no validity, cannot form the basis for any alteration of the status of [Crimea]." In 2016, the UN reaffirmed its non-recognition of the annexation and condemned "the temporary occupation of part of the territory of Ukraine – the Autonomous Republic of Crimea and the city of Sevastopol."

Besides the history of the Ukraine and Crimea, the distribution of ethnicities in the region had always been a confounding element in territorial disputes. Crimea has been a part of the Russian empire since 1783. In October 1921, the Crimean Autonomous Soviet Socialist Republic (ASSR) of the Russian Soviet Federative Socialist Republic (SFSR) was declared. After World War II, the Crimean ASSR lost its autonomy and became only an oblast, or province, of the Russian SFSR.

In 1954, the Crimean Oblast was realigned from the

Russian SFSR to the Ukrainian SFSR. In 1989, as part of Mikhail Gorbachev's *Perestroika* movement, the Crimean Tatars, a mostly Muslim ethnic group who had been deported by Stalin, were allowed to return to Crimea. In 1990, the Crimean Oblast proposed reconstituting the Crimean ASSR. The oblast conducted a referendum in 1991 to determine whether Crimea should be elevated into a union republic, but by that time the Soviet Union was in disarray and full collapse. The Crimean ASSR was restored for less than a year as part of Ukraine before it became independent from the Russian Federation. Ukraine recognized Crimea's autonomous status while the Supreme Council of Crimea affirmed the peninsula's "sovereignty" as a part of Ukraine.

On August 24th, 2009, ethnic Russian residents held demonstrations in Crimea. The predominant ethnicity in Crimea is Russian while there are significant minorities of both ethnic Ukrainians and Crimean Tatars. Nonetheless, demographically Crimea represents one of Ukraine's largest ethnic Russian populations. In a 2001 Ukrainian census, 90.6% of the population of Sevastopol indicated Russian as their primary language, followed in second place by Crimea at 77%. As academician William Varettoni had presciently stated in 2011, " . . . Russia wants to annex Crimea and is merely waiting for the right opportunity, most likely under the pretense of defending Russian brethren abroad."

In 2010, Viktor Yanukovych won election as President of Ukraine with firm backing from the Autonomous Republic of Crimea and both Southern and Eastern Ukraine. His supporters argued that those working against him were "threatening political stability in the country." They urged Crimeans to "strengthen friendly ties with Russian regions." On February 4th, 2014, the Presidium of Crimea's Supreme Council entertained conducting a referendum on the peninsula's status and sought Russia's support to guarantee the legitimacy of the vote. In response, the Ukrainian Security Service (SBU) opened a criminal investigation into Russia's possible "subversion" of Ukraine's territorial integrity. On February 20th, the Chairman of Crimea's Supreme Council visited Moscow where he proclaimed that the 1954 transfer of Crimea from Russia to Ukraine had been a mistake.

In January 2014, the Sevastopol city council called for the standing up of a "people's militia" to "ensure firm defense" of the city from "extremism". An unscheduled meeting of the Crimean parliament on February 21st was attacked by the Crimean Tatar community as nothing more than a pretext to call for Russian military intervention. This caused the SBU to announce that it would "use severe measures to prevent any action taken against diminishing the territorial integrity and sovereignty of Ukraine."

A new SBU chief requested the United Nations to

provide monitoring of the security situation in Crimea. At the same time, Russian troops seized the main road to Sevastopol on direct orders from Russian President Putin. On February 27th, Russian special forces took control of the building housing the Crimean Supreme Council. Soldiers raised a Russian flag atop the building and barricades were erected outside it. The parliament voted to terminate the existing Crimean government and replaced the sitting prime minister with Sergey Aksyonov, a member of the Russian Unity party.

Additionally, parliament voted to hold a referendum on greater autonomy for Crimea on May 25th. No independent journalists were permitted in the building during the vote and a number of the MPs claimed to have been threatened while votes were cast on their behalf and those who were not even present in the building. The Ukrainian press stated that "it is impossible to find out whether all the 64 members of the 100-member legislature who were registered as present [were there] when the two decisions were voted on or whether someone else used the plastic voting cards of some of them" due to the armed occupation of parliament. That same day, troops in uniform, again bearing no insignia, established security checkpoints on the Isthmus of Perekop and the Chonhar Peninsula which separate Crimea from the Ukrainian mainland. Thus, Crimea had essentially been cut off from Ukraine.

On March 1st, Prime Minister Aksyonov stated that

Crimea's new *de facto* government would take control of all the Ukrainian military installations on the peninsula. He also sought Russian President Putin's "assistance in ensuring peace and public order" in Crimea. Subsequently, Putin authorized Russian military intervention in Ukraine "until normalization of a socio-political environment in the country" could be achieved. Russian troops once again undertook operations in Crimea without insignia. By March 4th there were units of the 18th Motor Rifle Brigade, 31st Air Assault Brigade, and 22nd Spetsnaz Brigade deployed and operating in Crimea. Even as late as April 17th, Russian Foreign Minister Lavrov was claiming that there were no Russian armed forces in Crimea.

Finally, Russian President Putin acknowledged the presence of Russian military troops, but stated that Russia's intervention was necessary "to ensure proper conditions for the people of Crimea to be able to freely express their will." It was said that the military actions in Crimea were undertaken by forces of the Black Sea Fleet and were justified by the "threat to lives of Crimean civilians" and the danger of "takeover of Russian military infrastructure by extremists." Both the United States and the United Kingdom accused Russia of violating the provisions of written agreements by which Russia, the U.S., and the UK had pledged to refrain from the threat or use of force against the territorial integrity or political independence of Ukraine. However, by prior agreement with Ukraine, Russia was allowed to maintain up to 25,000 troops, 24 artillery systems (with a caliber smaller than 100 mm), 132 armored vehicles, and 22 military planes on military bases in Sevastopol and related infrastructure on the Crimean Peninsula. The Black Sea Fleet had basing rights in Crimea until 2042.

Under the terms of the Constitution of Russia, the admission of new federal subjects is governed by federal constitutional law. The law, adopted in 2001, sets forth that admission of a foreign state or its part into Russia shall be based on a mutual accord between the Russian Federation and the subject state and shall take place pursuant to an international treaty between the two countries. It also stipulates that the admission must be initiated by the state in question, not by anyone subdivision or by Russia itself. On February 28th, a Russian Member of Parliament, along with other members, introduced an amendment to alter Russia's procedure for adding federal subjects. The amendment stated that accession could be initiated by a subdivision of a country provided that there is an "absence of efficient sovereign state government in the foreign state." It also stipulated that the request could be made either by subdivision bodies on their own or on the basis of a referendum held in the subdivision in accordance with prevailing national law. On March 11th, both the Supreme Council of Crimea and the Sevastopol City Council adopted a declaration of independence stating their intent to exercise their independence and request full accession to Russia.

Ukraine's acting President, Oleksander Turchinov,

stated that "The authorities in Crimea are totally illegitimate, both the parliament and the government. They are forced to work under the barrel of a gun and all their decisions are dictated by fear and are illegal." On March 14th the Crimean referendum was deemed unconstitutional by the Constitutional Court of Ukraine. The referendum was held despite the opposition from the Ukrainian government and, not unexpectedly, the "official" results indicated that 95% of the participating voters in Crimea were in favor of being annexed by Russia.

Thus, the status of Crimea and its capital of Sevastopol were determined, if not settled. But Vladimir Putin had his eye on a much greater prize. Ukraine, with its 1,730 miles of coastline on the Black Sea, if added to Russia's holdings, would give them additional Black Sea ports, the most notable of which being Odessa, and a much shorter route through the Bosphorus to the Mediterranean than that from the Sea of Azov Northeast of Crimea. Finally, it would expand not only the territorial waters of Russia with the fishing and mineral rights which accompanied them but also its significant land mass above which it could legally declare an Air Defense Identification Zone, the better to defend the Motherland against incursion from the South.

Chapter Five

On Saturday, December 1st, 2018, Ukrainian President Petro Poroshenko reported to German Chancellor Angela Merkel that Russia was massing both land forces and weaponry along the Ukrainian border. In a show of support, Merkel admonished Russia not to blockade the Ukrainian ports of Mariupol and Mykolaiv in the Sea of Azov in far Eastern Ukraine. Tensions between Russia and Ukraine had continued to escalate ever since warships from the Black Sea Fleet fired upon three small Ukrainian naval vessels on November 25th and seized 24 of their crewmen.

At the G-20 Summit in Buenos Aires, Russian President Putin was asked about his aggressive actions and ultimate intentions. Putin squarely placed the blame for the confrontation upon Ukraine for violating Russian territorial waters. In response, the Ukrainian president accused Russia of deploying "more than 80,000 troops, 1,400 artillery and multiple rocket launch systems, 900 tanks, 2,300 armored combat vehicles, 500 aircraft, and 300 helicopters" along Ukraine's common border with Russia. If accurate, these figures would account for the vast majority of men and hardware assigned to Russia's Western Military District.

"The Kremlin is further testing the strength of the global order," Poroshenko said, speculating that Moscow was pushing its territorial limits further into Ukrainian territory while waiting to see if the international community would allow it to assert that the Sea of Azov and Black Sea are Russian territorial waters.

He also claimed that Russia was enhancing its military presence in both the Sea of Azov and the Black Sea. "In the waters of the Black Sea, Sea of Azov, and Aegean Sea," he said, "more than 80 ships and 8 submarines are on patrol – including 23 combat vessels . . ." As a response to Russia's firing on Ukrainian ships in November, Poroshenko had the Ukrainian parliament implement martial law in ten border regions. But many, both at home and abroad, feared that the martial law order would only antagonize Putin and was declared solely to benefit Poroshenko, who would be running for re-election in March, politically.

Officials in Ukraine were concerned that Russia may be preparing to escalate the conflict, even speculating that an offensive may originate in Crimea. They had accused Russian separatists of violating a so-called "New Year's Truce", attacking Ukrainian positions with a heavy-caliber weapon banned under the 2015 bilateral agreement. Positions in Ukraine were targeted using 120mm mortar rounds although the 2015 agreement banned weapons with a greater diameter than 100mm in a 50-kilometer zone running along the front line between Russia and Ukraine.

A Washington-based think tank, the Institute for the Study of War, had observed, "Russia continues to build up and prepare its military forces for possible offensive operations against Ukraine from the Crimean peninsula and the East." They indicated that Russian President Putin was simply trying to keep the West guessing. "The data suggests that Putin is preparing to attack, although alternative interpretations are possible," they continued. A senior European defense official told the Voice of America (VOA), "The unpredictability is the point. Putin is testing Ukraine and the West to see if he'll be checked, to see what he can get away with, and maybe with an eye to securing another summit early this year with [the U.S. President]."

Russia's redeployments and buildup of military troops have alarmed former commander of the U.S. Army Europe, Lieutenant General Ben Hodges. He has predicted that unless there is greater Western pushback, "they won't stop until they completely own the Sea of Azov and have choked out Ukraine's very important seaport of Mariupol. The next phase will probably be land and sea operations that would eventually secure maybe even Mariupol but continue to take the Ukrainian coastline and connect Crimea back up to Russia along the Sea of Azov. It's not going to happen in the next six months, but this is the direction they're taking until they completely own the Black Sea and they've isolated Ukraine." Although the United States has no formal military bases in Ukraine, it has established a sizable footprint in the region.

Notwithstanding the fact that Ukraine is not a member

of the North Atlantic Treaty Organization (NATO), many nations in the West have issued formal condemnations of Russia's actions in Ukraine. And while a direct U.S. – Russia confrontation had always been deemed unlikely, it had maintained troops and weaponry in Eastern Europe and the Black Sea region that could respond.

In Ukraine, the Tennessee National Guard's 278th Armored Cavalry Regiment has troops on the ground helping that country run its Yavoriv Combat Training Center, comparable to Fort Polk in Louisiana or Fort Irwin in California, which prepares Ukrainian troops for combat deployments. Additionally, the Army keeps a rotating armored brigade in Eastern Europe year-round. The 1st Brigade Combat Team, 1st Cavalry Division was just completing its rotation and awaiting the 1st Armored Brigade Combat Team, 1st Infantry Division. They are to be joined by the 4th Combat Aviation Brigade, 4th Infantry Division.

The Marine Corps in the area is attached to the Black Sea Rotational Force. This force consists of several hundred Marines and sailors who participate in security cooperation exercises across the region. However, the Marines who participated in the force had departed as part of their normally-scheduled rotation in September 2018.

While small, the Corps' presence in the Black Sea serves as a powerful deterrent against would-be aggressors because, being both mobile and agile, the Marines in the

Black Sea move rapidly around the region helping to train and advise partner forces to boost collective security. From July to September alone, they had initiated three training evolutions with partner forces in Ukraine, Romania, and Georgia.

The 2018 *Operation Sea Breeze* in Ukraine involved roughly 50 Marines with Echo Company, 2nd Battalion, 25th Marine Regiment. The operation enraged the Russians. "Military activities will take place in direct proximity to the conflict zone in Southeastern Ukraine where Ukrainian military units continue to shell peaceful Donbass cities every day despite a 'bread truce' announced on July 1 by the Minsk Contact Group," said Russian Foreign Ministry spokesperson Maria Zakharova during a July briefing. "Attempts to flex muscles in these conditions will hardly help stabilize the situation in this region."

As for the Air Force, it had also conducted significant exercises in Ukraine in 2018. The California National Guard has been seconded to Ukraine through a State Department partnership program since 1993, often rotating airmen through the country for training. That partnership had been escalated in 2018.

It had just recently concluded Operation *Clear Sky 2018*, a multinational air exercise hosted by Ukraine in October. "It was basically the largest of its kind in Eastern Europe ever," said Lieutenant Colonel Robert Swertfager, the partnership program director for the California Air National Guard. The exercise paired California Air National Guard units with the Ukrainian Air Force during close-air-support missions, cyberdefense operations, and air sovereignty defense drills. Also, as part of *Clear Sky 2018*, pararescuemen, colloquially known as pararescue jumpers or simply PJ's, from the 131st Rescue Squadron had trained their Ukrainian counterparts at Vinnytsia Air Base, Ukraine. Designed to promote peace, security, and interoperability between regional allies as well as NATO partners, the two-week exercise had brought together nearly 1,000 military personnel from nine countries.

The Air Force also has multiple air assets in Europe that fly reconnaissance and air sovereignty missions over NATO allies. One mission is Intelligence, Surveillance, and Reconnaissance (ISR) utilizing unarmed MQ-9 *Reaper* drones, which had begun ISR operations from Miroslawiec Air Base, Poland, in May 2018. "U.S. Air Forces in Europe regularly conducts exercises with allies and partners in the region, however, we do not currently have USAFE-assigned Airmen in Ukraine," said Lieutenant Colonel Petermann, an AFE spokesperson in Europe.

The Naples-based U.S. 6th Fleet doesn't maintain a permanent presence in the Black Sea, but it does maintain, on a rotational basis, warships and support vessels through the waterway. In Summer 2017, the *Ticonderoga* class guided-missile cruiser *Hué City* and the Ukrainian auxiliary ship *Balta* conducted search-and-seizure training during exercise *Sea Breeze*. The *Balta* served as a "non-compliant" vessel and it was boarded by *Hué City* sailors.

In 2018, the guided-missile destroyers *James E. Williams*, *Carney*, *Ross,* and *Porter* entered the Black Sea, making stops in Bulgaria and Romania in support of Operation *Atlantic Resolve*, a naval operation dedicated to NATO's collective defense of the Black Sea. The *Carney*, home-ported in Rota, Spain, also visited the Ukrainian port of Odessa. The *Harper's Ferry* class amphibious dock landing ship *Oak Hill* and the 26th Marine Expeditionary Unit transited the Dardanelles Strait to participate in the Romanian-led Operation *Spring Storm* exercise.

In May 2018, a detachment of the Sicily-based *Red Lancers* assigned to Navy Patrol Squadron 10 engaged their P-8A *Poseidon* planes to participate in NATO Maritime Group 2's *Sea Shield* exercise. In July, the 6th Fleet's flagship *Mount Whitney* entered the Black Sea to participate in the annual *Sea Breeze* exercise with Ukraine. The nations focused on maritime interdiction operations, air defense, anti-submarine warfare, damage control drills, search and rescue, and amphibious warfare.

In August, the Military Sealift-operated expeditionary fast transport ship *Carson City* arrived in Constanta, Romania, where it dropped off the U.S. Army's Bravo Company, 2nd Battalion, 5th Cavalry Regiment. The

Spearhead class vessel later shuttled soldiers and their equipment from Poti, Georgia, back to Romania. But the military tensions with Russia in the region have not been limited to maritime incidents such as the firing on three Ukrainian vessels and the capture of 24 crewmen.

In January, a Sukhoi SU-27 *Flanker* fighter intercepted a Navy EP-3 *Aries II* surveillance plane in international airspace over the Black Sea. The Pentagon characterized the interdiction as "unsafe" when the Russian pilot closed to within five feet of the Navy aircraft and veered into its flight path, forcing the turbo-prop plane to fly through the fighter's jet wash. Later, in November, the incident was repeated. Filmed footage of the incident shows a *Flanker* on the starboard side of a Greece-based Navy EP-3 *Aries II* banking right of its nose before the Russian pilot hit his afterburners, forcing the plane to fly through the turbulent air of the aircraft's jet wash.

Chapter Six

It was becoming increasingly evident to the well-trained eye that a full-scale invasion of Ukraine by Russia was precariously imminent. Both the Joint Chiefs of Staff and the American President, John Jefferson, were well-aware that every operation which the United States staged in Ukraine, or in which the U.S. military participated, was being closely monitored by plain-clothed Russian military operatives on the ground as well as by sensors and cameras strategically placed at critical crossroads and bridges throughout the country. Additionally, on successive passes, Russia's latest generation of reconnaissance satellites which were approaching, but had not yet achieved, the sophistication of America's KH-13 (KH for "Keyhole") ISR-gathering orbital platforms, was observing and recording the American military's every move in and around Ukraine.

The first generation of Russian spy satellites, which were in operation from 1961 until 1994, was named *Zenit*. The *Zenits* were succeeded by the real-time, digital *Yantar* generation of satellites which were in use from 1974 until 2015. Then followed the *Resurs DK* class of remote sensing satellites whose use spanned the years from 2006 until 2016. And, finally, on Thursday, February 7th, 2019, Russia had launched its newest spy satellite, named *Kosmos 2525*, atop a *Soyuz 2-1v* rocket from the Plesetsk Cosmodrome roughly 500 miles North of Moscow at 8:38PM Moscow time. The

Kosmos 2525 is a new, smaller-designed reconnaissance satellite capable of taking high-resolution surveillance imagery of the Earth's surface.

The implication of this monitoring is that, if the United States were to be called upon to assist Ukraine in defending its territorial integrity, the only way to seize the upper hand in the conflict would be to introduce assets not currently under Russian surveillance. Large troop movements could not be concealed, and surface warships, though lethal, were neither swift nor stealthy. This would leave any need for the element of surprise to come from the Air Force. Fortunately, they possessed assets which were not frequently the object of Russia's monitoring programs.

First, there is a significant U.S. Air Force presence at the Al Udeid Air Base in Qatar, 1,950 miles away from central Ukraine. Qatar is in the midst of spending $1.8 billion upgrading the base used by the United States for its ongoing military and counterterrorism operations in the Middle East and Afghanistan. Al Udeid houses 10,000 U.S. military personnel. More importantly, it is the provisional home to the Air Force's 379th Air Expeditionary Wing, part of the Air Combat Command, which has been pivotal in the war against terrorism with its air attacks on ISIS positions in Syria and Northern Iraq.

In addition to its fleet of KC-135 *Stratotankers* which extend the combat radius of all the Air Force's combat aircraft, it also houses a number B-52 *Stratofortress* bombers. But what makes it stand out, even more, is that it is currently host to a number of the Air Force's B-1B *Lancer* supersonic, variable-sweep wing, heavy bombers. The *Lancer's* top speed is classified but exceeds 830 mph, or Mach 1.25, and it has an operational ceiling in excess of 60,000 feet or 12 miles. It is half the length of a football field and its wingspan is variable from 79 to 137 feet. It has state-of-the-art avionics and most frequently carries 24 GBU-31 Joint Direct Attack Munition (JDAM) GPS-guided bombs with either MK-84 GP (General Purpose) warheads or BLU-109 hardened penetration "bunker buster" warheads.

2,500 hundred miles to the Northwest lies Aviano Air Base on the Northeast coast of Italy. It is a NATO base of which the Italian Air Force has ownership. Of critical importance in any air operations over Ukraine would be the 510th Fighter Squadron "Buzzards" and the 555th Fighter Squadron "Triple Nickel". Each is assigned 21 F-16 *Fighting Falcons*. Both squadrons are part of the 31st Fighter Wing headquartered at Aviano which is part of United States Air Force Europe.

The F-16 is a single-jet, supersonic, multirole fighter aircraft. It is the most prevalent air superiority, day fighter in use today, employed by numerous nations around the world from Bahrain to Belgium and from Thailand to the United Arab Emirates. To date 4,604 have been manufactured.

The aircraft is 50 feet long with a 39-foot wingspan. It is powered by a single afterburning, turbofan jet engine which produces a maximum speed in excess of 1,300 mph and an operating ceiling of over 50,000 feet with a 340-mile combat radius. From its hardpoints, it can launch 6 *Sidewinder* air-to-air missiles, 6 air-to-surface *Maverick* missiles, or 2 air-to-ship *Harpoon* missiles. It can also drop anywhere from 6 GBU-12 *Paveway II* laser-guided bombs to 4 Mark 82 general purpose bombs to B-61 and B-83 nuclear weapons.

Because of the combat radius of the F-16, the flight of 850 miles East to central Ukraine would require at least one mid-air refueling in each direction with the second being required immediately after flying into secure airspace after any prolonged aerial encounter. These refuelings could be provided by the *Stratotankers* out of Mildenhall in England. But then there was the wild card; Incirlik.

Incirlik Air Base is located in Adana, Turkey. It is best known as the base from which, in the 1950s and 1960s, the U.S. Air Force U-2 *Dragon Lady* reconnaissance jets flew to provide intelligence after overflying Russia which, because of their 70,000-foot+ ceiling, went undetected. In 1960, Francis Gary Powers was shot down by a surface-to-air missile above the Soviet Union causing an international incident.

From time to time the Air Force has flown F-15 *Eagle* twin-jet, all-weather, tactical fighter aircraft out of Incirlik. It has also launched the occasional F-22 *Raptor* fifth-generation, single-seat, twin-jet, all-weather, stealth tactical fighter aircraft for raids on ISIS positions throughout the Middle East. Finally, it has housed a fairly stable contingent of KC-135 *Stratotankers* to provide air-to-air refueling capabilities for all other Air Force aircraft in the region.

A problem, however, has been the somewhat erratic behavior of Turkey's President, Recep Erdoğan, who has wavered between seeking the support of Russian President Vladimir Putin and American President John Jefferson. When he is seeking Russia's support of the al-Assad regime in Damascus to suppress the advances and resurgence of the Syrian rebels, most pointedly the Kurdish rebels in Northern Syria, he puts limits on the use of Incirlik for American combat sorties over Syria. For even though Russia's espoused intent is to attack ISIS strongholds, the focus of their air campaigns has appeared to be targeted on the anti-al-Assad rebels.

By the same token, Turkey is a member of NATO. Article 5 of the NATO charter, invoked for the first time in the wake of the attacks on the Twin Towers on 9/11, calls for each member state to consider an armed attack against one member state, in either Europe or North America, to be an armed attack against each individual member and to respond accordingly. The time may come when the Erdoğan regime finds itself in need of NATO's support. Therefore, he must do his best to appease the United States as it is the single most powerful signatory to the NATO charter. His ambivalence, alternately between seeking the support of Russia and the support of the United States, makes his permission to use Incirlik as a base for offensive operations by the Americans somewhat unpredictable. He is walking a tightrope and, due to his unstable demeanor, depending upon access to Incirlik presents its own risks.

Thus, the Air Force planners of any offensive mission above Ukraine or, more likely, defensive mission in support of Ukraine's battle with Russia over its territorial integrity, can depend upon the assets in Qatar and Italy, but must be cognizant of the inconsistent access to Incirlik in Turkey when preparing any order of battle. Any plan must be flexible, taking into consideration the vagaries of Incirlik's availability and the Air Force must be agile enough in its planning to be able to respond at a moment's notice to changes in the battlefield environment. This is where the unique capabilities of Kessel Run will come into play.

Chapter Seven

By the Winter of 2019, Kessel Run had become an integral player in the planning and attendant logistics of any Air Force mission. Requests continuously came into the office on Portland Street for support in preparing for potential combat missions across the face of the globe. The reputation which they had built had proven that their input led to a school of comprehensive planning which took into account all possible anticipated contingencies.

Air Force Captain Bryon Kroger, Kessel Run's chief operating officer, had spoken at length about the historical remnants of the military's acquisition culture going back as far as World War II. "Culture is the hardest thing. One thing that's really hard is psychological safety. Something we talk a lot about is, how do you create an environment where people feel truly safe to fail? Making that happen is hard. Adam [Furtado, Kessel Run's chief of product] and I are both military, Colonel Oti is military, and we have these natural tendencies around command-and-control style organization, and we need the exact opposite of that."

At the time the air-to-air refueling program JIGSAW had been put into operation at the Air Force's AOCs worldwide, Northrop Grumman was already three years behind schedule on its contracted project to overhaul the AOCs' suite of software and the budget for the project had swollen from the original $375 million to a whopping $745 million. At that time, they were neither aware of Kessel Run's accomplishments, nor even its existence.

Northrup Grumman came back to the Air Force and told them that the budget for their work would once again have to be increased just as JIGSAW was being successfully implemented. While the airmen in AOCs were disposing of their whiteboards, the Air Force issued a "stop work" order to Northrop, directing them to engage in no more work on the contract. By June, the contract had been canceled.

The Air Force's Director of Programs at Defense Digital Service, Hunter Price, said, "I think the Air Force and the Hill (Capitol Hill) both realized that AOC 10.2 was not on a path to deliver anything, which made it pretty easy to let go." The Northrup project had called for enhancing the security and networking capabilities of the AOC software suite without rewriting the 43 apps that run on top of it. Kessel Run, on the other hand, had already begun to roll out a product encompassing lower-level functionality using event-driven architecture while allowing its development teams to access classified databases and securely distribute information to thousands of airmen.

According to Lieutenant Colonel Jeremiah Sanders, its Deputy Director, Kessel Run had only been budgeted for $68 million in Fiscal Year 2018. But he had expected that more money could be reallocated in the form of contracting instruments from DIUx and other sources. Raytheon, one of the military's largest contractors, had earned a $375 million contract to perform long term maintenance on the AOC software and had found itself working with Kessel Run engineers.

When Northrup's project was terminated, Sanders and Oti had their engineers look over the code which had already been delivered. Unfortunately, they were unable to incorporate any of it into the new system. "Just because you followed the software requirements spec doesn't mean you met the capability need," Captain Kroger said.

"There's a lot of fault to go around on all of this, and we're not sitting here trying to say the defense industrial base can't write good software," Oti said. "The requirements process that we are forcing on them, they're forced to build to what we asked them for, even if they know it's not the right thing."

Eric Schmidt told Congress, "The DoD violates pretty much every rule in modern product development." One thing in common in all the decision-making processes at Kessel Run, from that of starting their work at the low-level code stage to virtually any team decision, was that it was made on the run based upon the end user's needs at that moment. In the current environment in the software coding business, this represents one of the industry's best practices. But at DoD, agility such as that is customarily impossible.

Specs are written over the course of years, and by the time the code can be field-tested, it is frequently obsolete.

Colonel Oti said, "Kessel Run is not just about building applications. We within the DoD need to relook at how we do requirements. We have to be able to take these technical requirements decisions and move them down to that product level, versus at the acquisitions level." Much as with the software engineers, acquisition executives require the "psychological safety" which enables them to depart from the risk-averse DoD culture that has ensnared them in its bureaucratic red tape. "There's plenty of additional things that can be done, even without new authorities being granted," Schmidt has said. "But there's got to be cultural safety associated with doing that. It's interesting for the history books that our contribution was observation. And then we left, and somebody else did the work."

Former Secretary of Defense Ash Carter stated that one of the best ways to foster change is to "set the right example and don't try to do everybody's work for them. This isn't the kind of thing that it's useful to make people do." But DDS Director Chris Lynch said, "We believe that technical people need to be in the room making technical decisions in places of authority. Anything less than that will end up placing us back into the results we have right now."

"Hopefully, we're just the tip of the spear," Lieutenant Colonel Sanders said, "and the Department of Defense relooks at how we do requirements, budgeting, and the acquisition process for both software and hardware . . ." AFCENT Chief of Staff Colonel Drowley said, "We've been granted those authorities because we're a combatant command right now that's in wartime operations."

The Defense Innovation Board has stated, "But it shouldn't be necessary for us to rethink the Pentagon's business practices in the midst of a war, just so we can get our fighting forces a UI (user interface) that works – never mind a state-of-the-art fighter jet. It hasn't been peacetime in a long time."

In the beginning, it will look much like the military's program office for buying services. "It won't do all of the software development for the Air Force. There's no way it could," said Roper in a September 7th, 2018, interview. "But the hope is that it will be able to manage agile software development for some of the Air Force's most tricky programs, while at the same time providing expertise and software development tools to the rest of the program offices.

"As programs shift to agile development, where they're pushing code out every month, where they are working directly with the user, where they are measuring their output using metrics that tell them whether it's good code or bad code, PEO Digital will provide Air Force standards for doing it and a playbook for making it work."

"We're figuring out what's the right timeline for that piece of code being left with the operator and [whether] the operator's happy. How do you decide what's too big of an increment of code and break it up? It's stuff that we're going to have to have a standard process [for]. It won't be perfect on Day One. But we know the analog has worked well for service contracts. We just need to perfect the unique twist that software adds, starting with pathfinders that are low hanging but still impactful for the Air Force.

"How do you manage its lead and cycle times, velocity, backlog, and deficiency retirement so that the taxpayer and warfighter get quality code for their dollars? For services, you do that with good metrics. For instance, you know you're getting good IT support if you have enough bandwidth, don't have many outages and pay a fair market price."

The Air Force's Chief Technology Officer Frank Konieczny wants to make sure all of its tech deals mimic its agile software development model Kessel Run. "You're probably going to see maybe a directive from us that basically says every acquisition is going to have to have something that looks like Kessel Run from the primes. So you want to have [the authority to operate] within three or four weeks, not six years," he said in Pentagon City, Virginia on October 3rd.

The Air Force has been pushing for broad organizational change when it comes to adopting new technology, as evidenced by the newly launched digital program executive office (PEO) to handle agile software development. Marine Corps Brigadier General Dennis Crall, DoD's senior military advisor for cyberpolicy, said, "We spend a lot of time and frustration in the department trying to make disparate software applications communicate with each other. [Young workers are] screaming for ways to contribute, and we are taking that on board and showing great promise, but there's a lot of work ahead."

Konieczny said that in this case, the human element puts a kink in the long-term success of agile software development. To help address the issue, the Air Force is considering bringing back programming as a career field, but that won't solve everything. "You're going to have some turnover all the time, so the code has to be in such a way that you can pick it up and utilize it – putting some standardization across the code which will help push products out faster," he said.

"We shot for the moon and decided to take a page out of the Silicon Valley playbook," said Adam Furtado, Kessel Run's chief of product. *Bloomberg* has reported that DIUx – the Pentagon's experimental procurement group – worked with Air Force planners and a few Pivotal software developers "to set up a streamlined scheduling system in less than 120 days for $1.5 million."

Major General Zabel, the Air Force's director of the IT acquisition process development at the Pentagon, has said it's easy to *talk* about changing the culture. "But look around and you can see that these airmen are learning. They're building actual products, and they're writing the book on how to be combat engineers for the information age."

"A lot of different organizations are providing airmen to come and what's great is they come here and they provide value to us, and then we send them back to their units and now they're trained programmers that can solve problems within their unit," Captain Kroger said. "You'd come to them with a real problem to solve and you build real software that you deliver to real operations, in our case to the classified network at the Air Operations Center. They do paired programming where two engineers sit at the same terminal and code on a problem. And then we also pair our designers with a Pivotal designer and our product manager with a Pivotal product manager. And they work, eight hours a day, five days a week on this piece of software."

"We've established a culture where those developers and those operators are tied at the hip," Kroger said. "And that allows us to get our software out the door much faster, and to be able to run it more stable in production. If you're building a bridge, you don't want to change plans halfway through building the bridge," he said as an example. "But with software, it's cheap and relatively easy to make changes as you go."

The biggest shift for everyone to overcome, Kroger pointed out, is getting out of the mindset of defining the entire thing you want to build up front. Taking a minimum viable product approach "changes the game", which he explained as "don't try to build the 100 percent solution. Build a 10 percent solution, get it out there, get feedback, and iterate on it."

"And it's still hard, don't get me wrong, and we have a long way to go to be able to institutionalize this and make it the norm across the Air Force," he said. "But, yeah, there are policy barriers, there's security. You want to go fast but you still want to be secure, and that takes a lot of work as well. Through Kessel Run, the airmen learn and challenge each other, and are challenged by Pivotal's employees," Kroger said.

"I'll say there's no talent shortage in the Air Force," said Kroger. "Our airmen are incredible when we bring them into these labs and put them in this environment. I think number one is identifying people with a growth mindset, and airmen, in general, have a growth mindset . . . And so you put them in this environment and you get out of the way. When I say pushing, I mean pushing it into the hands of the users on the classified network for real operations. So it's changing the game on how the DoD builds and delivers software."

On Wednesday and Thursday, the 23rd and 24th of January, 2019, Kessel Run conducted a recruitment event in Boston. Their objective was to fill out their roughly 300 authorized positions from the initial staff of 90. In addition to engineers and coders, they hired product managers. Each manager would be assigned a software program. Their task would be to shepherd that product throughout the development process from conception to implementation.

"The Air Force is seeing, and I think we're one of the ones showing them, how important it is to create and sustain your own software," said Adam Furtado. "As with many small companies, our goal now is to hire the right people, expand our pipeline, and continue supporting the Air Force's software needs. It's an exciting time to come work for us. We're offering . . . the ability to work on extremely advanced systems."

The new staff was given a time frame of from two weeks to 30 days to report for work. This would allow most new staffers the requisite time to give their current employers notice as well as relocate if necessary. All the new employees were expected to be on board in Boston by Monday, February 25th, when Kessel Run had completed its move to the best known classified facility in downtown Boston where it would occupy an entire floor of a shared office building. The timing couldn't have been better.

Chapter Eight

Before dawn on the morning of Wednesday, February 27th, the fifth anniversary of the day on which Russian troops captured the Supreme Council of Crimea and strategic sites across the province, Russian troops in battle tanks and other vehicles rolled into Ukraine from both the Russian – Ukrainian border and the Crimean – Ukrainian border. They included 120mm 2S9 *Nona* light-weight, self-propelled mortar tanks, 152mm 2S35 *Koalitsiya-SV* self-propelled howitzer tanks, and both 152mm 2S19 *Msta/S2S19M1* and 2S19M2 *Msta/MS2* self-propelled howitzer tanks.

These powerful vehicles were backed up by echelons of T-90 third-generation main battle tanks. Behind them came several 122mm *Tornado-G* multiple rocket launchers, 9K720 *Iskander-M* tactical ballistic missile launchers capable of firing projectiles with 480kg conventional warheads 500 kilometers, and, finally, 2K22 *Tunguska* tracked, self-propelled anti-aircraft weapons armed with both surface-to-air guns and surface-to-air missile systems (SAMs).

The offensive launched from the far Eastern Ukrainian border headed due West for the heart of Ukraine. That which crossed the border to the Northwest had Kharkiv as its target. The city has a population of 1.5 million people making it Ukraine's second largest city, and it is home to the massive Annunciation Cathedral with 5 domes and a bell tower. The attack from due North headed South-southwest for Kiev, the Ukrainian capital, while the offensive from Crimea proceeded West-northwest toward Odessa, Ukraine's third most populous city and home to its Western Naval Base where the Headquarters of the Ukrainian Navy is located and the bulk of the Navy's fighting ships are homeported.

It was only 21 miles from the border to Kharkiv, and 160 miles to Kiev from the point where the Russian troops had crossed into Ukraine, but a more circuitous 160 miles from Crimea to Odessa. The forces advancing from the East would set up the operational headquarters for Russia's re-annexation of Ukraine in the center of the country in the city of Kropyvnytskyi, formerly Kirovohrad, midway between Kiev and Odessa and 370 miles West of Ukraine's Eastern border.

Russia's air operations in central Ukraine would be coordinated out of the Kryvyi Rih International Airport (KWG) 75 miles Southeast of Kropyvnytskyi which the ground forces approaching from the East had captured on their trek from the Eastern Ukrainian border. The airfield consisted of one concrete runway which ran due North and South and was 8,202 feet long. Thus, it could handle Russia's MiG-31 and Su-57 fighters as well as its Tu-22M and Tu-160 bombers, all of which would provide the ground troops with air support as needed. For operations close to the Russian or Crimean borders, air support would come from airfields on Russian or Crimean soil. The airfield in Crimea was oriented nearly due North and South and was over 12,000 feet long.

As for the Russian Navy, its role would be of a defensive nature, keeping foreign military vessels and aircraft from intruding upon Ukrainian territorial waters or airspace. Sailing from Sevastopol on the Crimean peninsula and Novorossiysk located East of the mouth of the Sea of Azov, Russian Navy guided missile destroyers, cruisers, and frigates from the 30th Surface Ship Division of the Black Sea Fleet and guided missile corvettes from its 41st Missile Boat Brigade would keep enemy surface vessels, as well as fighters and bombers, from staging an incursion into what was deemed nothing more than a renegade republic.

At 6:17AM, 7:17AM in Moscow and 9:17PM in the evening on Tuesday the 26th in Washington, the private phone rang in the residence of Ukrainian President Petro Poroshenko in the Mariyinsky Palace in Kiev. It was Colonel General Serhiy Popko, Commander of the Ukrainian Ground Forces, their equivalent of an army.

"Mister President! Mister President!" he began. "Russian ground troops and artillery have crossed into Ukrainian territory in the North, not far from Kiev, in the Northeast near Kharkiv, in the South from Crimea, and on the Eastern front. You must evacuate immediately, and we must put all of our 200,000+ ground forces on alert. Three of the targeted areas appear to be Kiev, Kharkiv, and Odessa. The fourth element of the invading force seems to be headed toward the physical heart of the nation, exact destination unknown."

"Serhiy," responded Poroshenko, "calm yourself. Did we not warn NATO and the Americans that this might happen? You have my permission to place the ground forces on alert. I will call President Jefferson in Washington and tell him of what has happened. And then my security detail and I will leave Kiev for a more secure location. Do not do anything precipitous until you hear back from me."

"But must we not confront this aggression head on?" asked General Popko. "We cannot permit them to make any progress on the ground! We must stop them in their tracks."

"Serhiy," said Poroshenko in a tone which made it clear he was frustrated with his general, "If our ground forces attack advancing Russian ground troops without the proper support, they will be slaughtered. We must coordinate with the Americans. I will inform the American President and he will send us help. Their air forces are more than a match for the Russians, and the new guns and missiles on the American warships will easily be able to target the Russian troops advancing on Odessa, even from the distance required to avoid direct confrontation with what, most certainly, must now be a cordon of Russian warships of the Black Sea Fleet off our Southern coast."

"As you wish, Mister President," conceded Popko. "But please make sure that the American commander of the operation contacts me at once. We must begin to formulate a plan to put down this despicable act of aggression."

"I will, Serhiy," said Poroshenko. "But I must now call Washington and then flee the capital before it is overrun. You will hear from both the American commander and me as soon as our military response is assured."

"Very well, Mister President. Goodbye." And with that Popko hung up. Poroshenko then got the switchboard on the line and ordered them to get him the American President Jefferson on the phone no matter how long it took.

John Jefferson was aboard Air Force One on a return flight to Washington from Dekalb, Illinois where he had just delivered a boisterous speech in support of his most recent steps in controlling illegal immigration across America's Southern border. It had been well-received by a sympathetic audience of like-minded Americans. The only detractors were a handful of protesters outside, all of them students from Northern Illinois University, carrying signs and chanting anti-Jefferson slogans.

When the phone call was received aboard Air Force One, it was immediately put through to Jefferson's onboard residential quarters.

"Petro," said the President, "this is John Jefferson. You caught me on my plane. What can I do for you?"

President Poroshenko proceeded to tell Jefferson what little he knew. When he was done, Jefferson paused for several moments before responding. He was compiling in his mind a list of those he would have to wake up in Washington and have them convene an emergency meeting of the Joint Chiefs at the Pentagon before sunrise Wednesday.

"Mister President," said Jefferson finally, "I am going to get my senior military leaders on this immediately. By noon tomorrow, we will call a meeting of my National Security Council (NSC) in the Situation Room at the White House. When that meeting concludes, I will call you with a battle plan which we, together, will be able to carry out and which you will be able to share with your commanders. Make sure I have a way of immediately contacting you at any time of the day or night."

"Thank you, Mister President," said Poroshenko. "And please have one of your senior military leaders call Colonel General Popko, the Commander of my Ground Forces, and brief him in. He is beside himself and in need of reassurance from America."

"Will do, Petro," said Jefferson. "I have to go now. There's much to be done." He hung up the phone and summoned his senior military officers to the conference room so that they could discuss available military assets in the area as well as offensive options in support of Ukraine's out-manned and out-gunned troops. He also directed his Chief of Staff to get in touch with the Chairman of the Joint Chiefs in Washington and tell him to get his team together in the conference room adjacent to his office on the ultra-secure E-ring of the Pentagon ASAP.

When General Mark Milley was contacted, he had one of his aides call the entire complement of the Joint Chiefs and instruct them to be in his conference room at the Pentagon at 0400 hours Wednesday morning. He also instructed the aide to place calls to both Bryon Kroger and Adam Furtado from Kessel Run and inform them that an Air Force C-21A, the military version of the Learjet 35, would be placed at their disposal at Hanscom Field outside of Boston to bring them to Washington. A staff car would pick them up at Andrews Air Force Base and transport them to the Pentagon. Subsequently, they would be accompanying the Joint Chiefs to a meeting of the National Security Council at the White House.

The meeting of the Joint Chiefs, with Kroger and Furtado in attendance, commenced on time. Assets were identified and scenarios proposed. Kroger and Furtado were interrogated to determine what skills Kessel Run could bring to the table. In addition to JIGSAW, RAVEN, and CHAINSAW, they told the chiefs they stood ready to provide the Air Operations Centers at both Aviano and Al Udeid with whatever new apps they might need to implement any operational plan upon which they might settle.

General Milley thanked them, in advance, for their commitment and told them he wanted them at the NSC meeting in the White House later in the day so that they could speculate on ways in which to enhance whatever missions were selected. It seemed that the consensus was to bring in the *Fighting Falcons* from Aviano and the *Lancers* from Al Udeid. Were there any *Raptors* at Incirlik, they would join the fight if permitted to take off by the Turkish president. Air-to-air refueling for the Aviano aircraft would be provided by the 100th Air Refueling Wing (ARW) out of RAF Mildenhall in England while that for the *Lancers*, if needed, would be supplied by the 340th Expeditionary Air Refueling Squadron (EARS), also flying out of Al Udeid. The mission of all the offensive warplanes would be to interdict the march of the Russian elements which would not only take out some of their weaponry but slow their progress in reaching their objectives. It would also give the Ukrainian Ground Forces more of a fighting chance against the superior Russian assets than if they were allowed to proceed unimpaired.

The USS *Harry S. Truman* (CVN-75), the eighth

Nimitz class carrier to be built, was currently assigned to the 6th Fleet. It was the lead ship of Carrier Strike Group 8 and the head of Task Force 60 headquartered in Naples, Italy. Accompanied by Destroyer Squadron 60 and Task Force 61 amphibious assault force which would be transporting Task Force 62, the landing force of the Marine expeditionary unit, the formation would head due East. At the Eastern end of the Mediterranean, they would pass through the Strait of the Dardanelles into the Sea of Marmara, then on through the Bosphorus Strait, and finally into the Black Sea. They would receive their orders en route.

The task of keeping all the aircraft in the operation both in the air and well-supplied with ordnance would principally be the job of their respective AOCs, but Kessel Run's apps would see that both tasks were conducted as efficiently and quickly as possible. Because of the need for the two AOCs to coordinate potentially overlapping responsibilities, Kessel Run would be required to cobble together an app in record time to keep all the warplanes fully armed and adequately fueled.

During the meeting of the Joint Chiefs, a mix of both breakfast staples and sandwiches had been delivered from the cafeteria. All in attendance ate as they spoke or listened. There would be no time for a leisurely meal before they piled into their fleet of staff cars with a military escort to facilitate their trip over the Potomac on Memorial Bridge and on to the White House for their 10:00AM NSC meeting.

Chris Knowles

Chapter Nine

As the attendees for the National Security Council meeting arrived at the White House, the Joint Chiefs and two men from Kessel Run were joined by the Secretary of State, as well as the Directors of the Central Intelligence Agency and National Security Agency. After they showed their IDs to the Marine guards and surrendered all of their electronic devices, they entered the Situation Room, the 5,525 square-foot secure conference room in the subbasement of the White House's West Wing.

As the visitors entered the room, they were greeted by President Jefferson and his National Security Advisor, Winifred "Winnie" Winstead. Everyone took their seat and the President called the meeting to order. He then turned the proceedings over to General Milley to get things started.

"Mister President, Ladies and Gentlemen," began the general, "just over twelve hours ago ground troops from the Russian Federation rolled across the Ukrainian border in four locations. Three of their targets appear to be Kiev, Kharkiv, and Odessa. The fourth seems to be somewhere in central Ukraine where they will be setting up their operational headquarters. Daylight imagery from our KH-13 *Misty* surveillance satellites reveals that each formation includes tanks, heavy artillery, and surface-to-air missile launchers. It has also revealed that warships from the

Russian Black Sea Fleet have formed a protective cordon along the Southern coast of Ukraine in the international waters of the Black Sea. Their role would appear to be defensive, warding off any intrusion by enemy forces approaching from the Med. As a preparatory gesture, I have ordered Carrier Strike Group 8, Destroyer Squadron 60, and Task Force 61 amphibious assault force which will be transporting Task Force 62, the landing force of the Marine expeditionary unit, to depart their homeport of Naples and get underway East for the Bosphorus." General Milley then turned the meeting back over to the President.

Jefferson looked to his right at the Secretary of State, retired Navy Admiral Charles Wainwright, and said, "What have you got for us on the diplomatic front, Mister Secretary?"

"Thank you, Mister President," said Wainwright. "As early as December, the Ukrainians reported to us that the Russians were massing troops on their side of the Ukrainian border. At that point, they had made no threatening gestures. We registered our displeasure with this situation with both the Russians and the UN Security Council. The Russians explained the actions away as nothing more than regularly scheduled military exercises. No one believed them, but then no one had any proof to the contrary.

"This morning I placed a call to my opposite number in Russia, Foreign Minister Sergey Lavrov, and registered both our alarm and displeasure at their military forces crossing into the sovereign territory of one of their former republics. His response was that the Russian Federation considered Ukraine nothing more than a renegade republic, much as the People's Republic of China views Taiwan, and that the move was designed as a first step in subduing them in preparation for re-annexation much as took place in Crimea five years ago today."

"That hardly seems a coincidence," said Jefferson. "Why is it that so many of our adversaries, from the Russians to ISIS, put so much stock in the somewhat mystical significance of the anniversaries of prior defeats or victories?"

"It's a cultural thing," said Wainwright. "Older cultures seem to believe that such actions serve as a way to either avenge a prior defeat or celebrate a prior victory. Lavrov made no allusion to Crimea, but that does not mean that President Putin did not have it on his mind when he gave the order to invade."

"What are we hearing from our allies?" asked Jefferson.

"I've heard from Germany, France, and the United Kingdom. They have all condemned Russia's actions and registered their displeasure with Lavrov. Also, while it should be noted that Ukraine is a member of neither, less than a week ago, on February 19th, Ukrainian President Poroshenko signed a constitutional amendment committing it to become a member of both NATO and the European Union. In a speech to their parliament, he said he saw Ukraine's becoming a member of those two organizations as his personal 'strategic mission'. He went on to say Ukraine should 'submit a request for EU membership and receive a NATO membership action plan no later than 2023.' In response, Donald Tusk, the President of the European Council, stated unequivocally that 'there can be no Europe without Ukraine.'"

"Then I'd say we have the tacit approval of both the EU and our NATO allies to take whatever measures necessary to secure Ukraine's independence," said Jefferson. "Winnie, I mean Ms. Winstead," he corrected himself, "what say you?"

"Thank you, Mister President," she started. "Ukraine has long been a thorn in Russia's side. Not only does it constitute a large land mass, but its lengthy coastline on the Black Sea is practically irresistible.

"For hundreds of years, Russia has been obsessed with access to warm water ports. Right now, Russia's only access to the Mediterranean is by navigating both the Sea of Azov and the Kerch Strait before reaching the Black Sea. Then it's 450 miles to the Bosphorus Strait and another 200 miles through the Sea of Marmara and the Strait of the

Dardanelles before they reach the Med. Sailing from Odessa would shave 100 miles off the journey. The military, much less commercial, value of annexing Ukraine is incalculable."

"OK," said President Jefferson, "I think I've heard enough. But, before I go on, I see two faces here this morning which I've never seen before. Would someone please introduce us?"

"They're with me," said Air Force Chief of Staff General David Goldfein. "The man in uniform is Captain Bryon Kroger, Chief Executive Officer of the Kessel Run Experimentation Lab in Boston, and the man to his left is Adam Furtado, Kessel Run's Chief of Product."

"And why are they here with us this morning?" asked the President.

"Sir," replied Goldfein, "Project Kessel Run is a lab in Boston where the best coders and engineers the Air Force can find work day and night on software programs and applications to be used by our Air Operations Centers around the world to keep our planes flying and to assure, as best we can, that we know what we want to hit, hit it with the greatest accuracy possible, and have the weaponry on hand to destroy it. They push out programs in weeks rather than years as did our previous commercial software vendors."

"Kessel Run, Kessel Run," pondered the President for a moment. "Is that Kessel Run as in Stars Wars, the *Millennium Falcon*, Han Solo?"

"That's the one, Sir," replied Goldfein.

"I like it. And now I think I remember reading an article about it on the Web," said Jefferson. "Well, Gentlemen, if you're as good as General Goldfein and your press says you are, Welcome!"

"They are, Sir," chimed in Goldfein.

"Thank you, Sir," said Kroger and Furtado in unison.

"Then let's get to work," resumed Jefferson. "We've got assets in Italy and Qatar ready to go. And, with any luck, we can use what we have on the tarmac at Incirlik. Have Carrier Strike Group 8 and its armada make all due speed for the Black Sea. We've got an ally to rescue and the clock is running. I'd hate to see Ukraine not make it to NATO.

"You all have your work cut out for you," concluded the President. "This meeting is adjourned."

Chapter Ten

At the conclusion of John Jefferson's National Security Council meeting, all of the participants dispersed to the locations where they would spend the bulk of their time during the Ukrainian crisis save the President himself. The Joint Chiefs and their Chairman boarded their staff cars for the return trip to the Pentagon where they would be camped out for an indefinite period. The Secretary of State, however, decided to take advantage of the break in the cold, slushy Winter weather and decided to take a leisurely stroll, accompanied by six of his Diplomatic Security Service (DSS) detail and his heavily armored black Suburban, back to the State Department building in Washington's Foggy Bottom.

Captain Bryon Kroger and Adam Furtado were given a ride back to Andrews in one of the numerous Secret Service vehicles parked at the White House where they would board the waiting Air Force Learjet for their return flight to Hanscom Field outside of Boston. From there, an Air Force staff car would take them to Kessel Run's offices downtown. The Directors of the CIA and NSA took their secure limousines back to Langley and Fort Meade respectively. And National Security Survivor Winnie Winstead took the elevator up to her office just down the hall from the Oval Office on the West Wing's second floor.

Only the President did not return to his office. He went, instead, to the main bedroom of the Presidential residence on the second floor of the central building where he took a brisk, refreshing cold shower, put on a fresh outfit of casual clothes, and had a hearty lunch before going to the Oval Office. He was in it for the long haul. And he had told his Appointments Secretary to cancel all his appointments for the day. He had also told his Press Secretary to inform the White House press corps that he would be conducting a press conference at 3:30PM. That would give him time to draft and polish an opening statement regarding the Russian invasion of Ukraine and then don a business suit for the network television cameras.

When the Joint Chiefs got back to their respective E-ring offices in the Pentagon, the Air Force Chief of Staff, Chief of Naval Operations (CNO), and Marine Corps Commandant all got on the phone to their forward commanders in the Ukrainian region and theater of operations. The Air Force's General Goldfein had his staff put together a conference call on a secure line with the Commanders of the Air Force units in Aviano, Al Udeid, and Incirlik. They included Brigadier General Daniel T. Lasica of the 31st Fighter Wing at Aviano, Brigadier General Jason R. Armagost of the 379th Air Expeditionary Wing at Al Udeid, and Colonel Davis S. Eaglin of the 39th Air Base Wing at Incirlik. When the four men had been connected, Goldfein began.

"Dan, Jason, Davis, this is Dave Goldfein at the Pentagon. As I'm sure you are all aware, this morning Russian troops rolled across the Ukrainian border on their way to Kiev, Kharkiv, Odessa, and central Ukraine where we suspect they'll be setting up their operational headquarters. There will, no doubt, be an airfield nearby where the Russian Air Force will establish its base of operations.

"The Ukrainian President asked President Jefferson for our help. As I see it, we will have two tasks. The first will be to destroy any and all Russian military aircraft on the ground as well as Russian military vehicles throughout the country. This will, no doubt, be made more difficult by the fact that the ground troops will embed themselves and their vehicles within the civilian neighborhoods of the cities which they capture.

"Secondly, we will be required to engage Russian aircraft in air-to-air combat in an effort to suppress their capability to strike Ukrainian military strongholds anywhere in their country. To accomplish these two tasks we will need both bombs and aircraft armed with air-to-air weapons. Dan, until the USS *Harry S. Truman* can make its way to the Black Sea, the air-to-air combat will fall predominantly to the *Fighting Falcons* of the Buzzards and Triple Nickel of the 510th and 555th. Air-to-air refueling will be provided by the 100th Air Refueling Wing out of Mildenhall."

"Understood, Sir," was all General Lasica of the 31st

Fighter Wing said.

"Jason, I want your B-1B *Lancers* to provide the heavy bombing. The *Lancers* carry more ordnance tonnage than any other aircraft in our arsenal or, for that matter, any aircraft in our history. Your refueling will be provided by the 340th EARS.

"Finally, Davis, I want you to have all your available F-22 *Raptors* at the ready to assist Dan. I know your status is tenuous, and that when President Erdoğan gets wind of the fact that you're flying combat missions against the Russian Air Force, he may well simply shut you down altogether. But until then, we need your firepower and agility. Should he close the base to American operations while your *Raptors* are in the air, we'll get you refueled by either the 100th or the 340th until we can get your aircraft safely on the ground at either Aviano or Al Udeid."

"We'll do our best not to let you down," said Colonel Eaglin.

"Good," continued Goldfein. "I've got the coders at Kessel Run putting together an app that will ensure that you've got the ordnance you need to do the job when and where you need it. They're also working on a modification of JIGSAW for you, Davis. Since Erdoğan is so unpredictable, we'll need to be able to adapt to the fluid circumstances while your aircraft are in the air. Just tell your pilots we've got the best coders in the Air Force working on it and that we won't leave them stranded with an empty gas tank."

"Will do, Sir," said Eaglin.

Down the hall, the CNO, Admiral John M. Richardson, was getting Rear Admiral Gene Black, the Commander of Carrier Strike Group 8 aboard the USS *Harry S. Truman*, the flagship of Task Force 60, on a secure line. The Air Force would be anxiously awaiting their arrival in the Black Sea accompanied by their contingent of Marines from the Marine expeditionary unit, Task Force 62. When Admiral Black was finally on the line, the CNO began.

"Gene, it's John Richardson here. I just got back from the White House where the President conducted a meeting of the NSC in the Situation Room. He's assured the Ukrainian President that we will render all available assistance in their defense against the Russian invaders. They're setting up in Kiev, Kharkiv, and Odessa, as well as in some central Ukrainian operations center. We're expecting the Russian Air Force to join them shortly and the Black Sea fleet to cordon off Ukraine's Southern coast.

"Our Air Force will be flying *Fighting Falcon* fighter missions out of Aviano and *Lancer* bomber missions out of Al Udeid. They'll also be bringing in some *Raptors* from

Incirlik if Erdoğan will let them fly. By the time you're in position in the Black Sea, we are hoping that the majority of bombing will be completed. But we'll still be in the thick of the air-to-air combat. We'll be able to supplement Aviano's *Fighting Falcons* with your F-18 *Super Hornet* multirole fighters as well as your contingent F-35C *Lightning II* stealth multirole fighters which will be certified as combat ready on Thursday as a result of their final trials aboard the USS *Carl Vinson*.

"While the U.S. will have plenty of F-16s and F-18s in the air, the stealthy nature of the *Raptors* and *Lightning IIs* will allow them to more safely go where the risk of detection by surface-to-air missiles and other combat aircraft is the highest.

"I also want you to get the USS *Mount Whitney* amphibious command ship as close in to Odessa as possible. Commandant Neller of the Marine Corps is probably in his office down the hall right now talking to the commander of his 2,000-Marine expeditionary unit telling him to prepare for an amphibious landing on the Ukrainian shoreline just East and West of Odessa. From their positions on the beaches, they should be able to execute a pincer movement and rout the Russian troops occupying the city.

"That's it for now, Gene," concluded Richardson. "Check in with my watch commander every six hours to keep us apprised of your progress toward the Bosphorus."

"That's a 'Roger', Admiral," said Clark.

As usual, Richardson had been right on the money. Marine Corps Commandant General Robert B. Neller was just finishing up his phone call with both the captain of the *Mount Whitney* and the commander of the Marine expeditionary unit. He had informed them to prepare for an amphibious landing on Ukraine's Southern shore. He had assured them that he would transmit all available satellite imagery of the area to their ultra-sophisticated comm center as soon as it became available and that their intelligence feed would, once they transited the Bosphorus Strait, be maintained in real time for the remainder of their mission.

While the world press continued to tout the rapid growth and increase in sophistication of the Chinese People's Liberation Army, the only fighting force in the world which could give the Americans a run for their money were the Russians. Ironically, after a Cold War spanning nearly half a century, it appeared that Americans would finally be shooting at Russians, and vice versa. While the object of the conflict, the former Soviet republic of Ukraine, seemed insignificant in the scheme of things, the outcome of the conflict would have worldwide and long-lasting ramifications.

Chris Knowles

Chapter Eleven

At 2:45PM, the President returned to the residence to freshen up and put on the business suit and tie which his personal steward had laid out for him. Because it was still Winter, he would be wearing a muted, charcoal gray herringbone tweed suit with a white shirt and muted paisley tie. Once dressed, he took a seat at the writing desk in the parlor and did one last run-through of his opening remarks.

At 3:20 he exited the residence, took the elevator down to the first floor, and headed for the White House press briefing room in the West Wing. At 3:28 he approached the podium and spent the next ninety seconds shuffling his notes. At 3:30 and thirty seconds the red light came on the pool camera trained on the podium, and, being broadcast on ABC, NBC, CBS, CNN, and Fox, he began.

"Ladies and Gentlemen, as I am sure most of you are aware, this morning before dawn local time Russian troops in heavy artillery rolled across the Ukrainian border in four locations. Three of their objectives appeared to be Kiev, Kharkiv, and Odessa. Our intelligence, surveillance, and reconnaissance satellites have yielded imagery which indicates that their fourth is somewhere in central Ukraine.

"Shortly thereafter, I received a phone call from the Ukrainian President, Petro Poroshenko, requesting that we assist him in driving back the Russian invaders and help him in ensuring his nation's territorial integrity. What many of you may not know is that, less than a week ago, he addressed his own parliament and told them that it is his sincerest desire to see Ukraine become a member of both the European Union and NATO. While we are not duty bound to come to the aid of Ukraine, I see it as our mission to help in the defense of any potential NATO member.

"We have aircraft in Italy, Qatar, and Turkey which can render immediate assistance. We have Carrier Strike Group 8 led by the USS *Harry S. Truman*, accompanied by U.S. Navy vessels including an amphibious command ship with 2,000 Marines on board, in the Mediterranean which is headed for the Black Sea off the Southern coast of Ukraine. Their aircraft can assist our Air Force while the Marines can help re-capture Odessa.

"The Russian aggression to re-annex a former Soviet republic which is now a sovereign nation must be stopped. The result of failure would be to set a precedent which their President Putin could use in an attempt to reconstitute the former Soviet Union. This cannot be allowed to happen, and his actions today must not be allowed to stand.

Consequently, our armed forces will render all possible aid and assistance to Ukraine. Their independence must be maintained. And, in the realm of international diplomacy, our friendship and alliance must be preserved to ensure political stability in the region.

"I will now take questions."

Pointing to the reporters in the front, Jefferson called out, "John Roberts, Fox, what's your question?"

"Thank you, Mister President," began Roberts. "You said that the invasion began before dawn this morning. Are you aware that today is the fifth anniversary of the Russian Federation's re-annexing of Crimea? And, if so, do you attribute any significance to this seeming coincidence?"

"I do, indeed, John," said Jefferson. "From terrorists to military tacticians, people in the so-called 'Old World' seem to ascribe some mystical significance to anniversaries of prior victories or defeats, either to celebrate the victories or avenge the defeats."

"A follow-up if I may please, Sir?" said Roberts.

"Sure, John, go ahead," said the President.

"Have you spoken to Russian President Vladimir Putin yet?" asked Roberts.

"I have not," said Jefferson. "For obvious reasons, I cannot, and will not, go into all the sources and methods of our intelligence collection process. But when I get Putin on the phone, I want to be armed with every detail of this invasion which our ISR people and technology can provide me. I want no surprises. And I want Putin to understand that we know every move that the Russians make, be it overt or covert. Next question?"

"Yes, Ms. Vega, ABC," said Jefferson.

"You stated that, as of now, Ukraine was neither a member of the European Union nor NATO," she began. "Do you think it's fair to ask American sailors, airmen, and Marines to risk their lives in defense of a nation, a former Soviet republic no less, to which we have no obligation?"

"Ms. Vega," the President responded, "In November of 2016, the American people elected me to be President. In doing so, they also chose me as this nation's Commander-in-Chief. This morning I conducted an emergency meeting of the National Security Council. In attendance were the Joint Chiefs, the Secretary of State, the Directors of the CIA and NSA, and the National Security Advisor, Ms. Winstead.

"We discussed this situation at length. At the end of the meeting, I announced my intentions. There was no dissent," concluded the President.

"But Mister President," interrupted Vega, "everyone you just mentioned was an individual whom you appointed. It's not surprising that they all agreed with you. But . . ."

Now President Jefferson, clearly antagonized, interrupted her, and in a much louder voice.

"Next question?" he said.

"Yes, Mark," said Jefferson, "What's your question?"

Cecilia Vega of ABC had continued to talk, but the microphone had been pulled away from her and both the President and Mark Knoller, the Chief White House Correspondent from CBS were talking over her. She eventually gave up and sat back down.

"Mister President," asked Knoller, "will we be joined by any of our NATO allies in this undertaking?"

"That's a good question, Mark," said Jefferson. "I can tell you that senior officials from the United Kingdom, France, and Germany had registered their alarm with Sergey Lavrov, the Russian Foreign Minister, before our NSC meeting took place this morning. I am also sure that many others have weighed in since. Each of will, of course, make a *formal* complaint to the UN Security Council.

"But, as of right now, the United States is the only country to have made a commitment of military assistance. The coordination of a military offensive of this size takes both massive and minute management. Our engagements and near misses with Russian aircraft over Syria in recent years have proven that.

"In the end, I expect this to be an air war. That means, if you see an aircraft which is not American, you may safely assume that it is Russian. We will even be asking that the Ukrainian Air Force limit its flights to those transporting troops or weaponry and that they maintain low altitudes. Too many aircraft in a small space sporting similar designs and numerous insignia is a recipe for disaster. Unless this conflict pours out beyond the borders of Ukraine, I believe it can best be prosecuted by U.S. military aircraft in conjunction with the Marine expeditionary forces which will work in cooperation with the Ukrainian ground forces. Time for one last question."

"Kristen," said Jefferson as he pointed to Kristen Welker, NBC's Chief White House Correspondent.

"Mister President," she began, "what do you envision as the End Game of this foray into adventurism on the part of the Russians?"

"Total and unconditional victory on the part of the Ukrainians and Americans. And total withdrawal on the part of the Russians. We will settle for nothing less."

And, with that, the President walked away from the podium and the press conference was over.

Chapter Twelve

As John Jefferson exited the briefing room, he took the stairs to the West Wing's second floor rather than taking his customarily short elevator ride. He wanted to blow off some steam and get his mind right for his next task. Before the press conference, the President had ordered his Communications Director to arrange for a telephone call to Russian President Vladimir Putin to be placed at 10:00PM Eastern time, 6:00AM in Moscow.

When he entered the Oval Office, he found two folders, both marked "Top Secret", sitting on top of the *Resolute* desk. One contained both a synopsis of the history between the Russian Federation and Ukraine following the fall of the Soviet Union as well as the latest intelligence take by both satellite and human assets on the ground relative to the Russian invasion over the past 18+ hours.

The second folder contained a summary of all of the military assets available in the region which the President could bring to bear on the Russian troops, aircraft, and warships. It also contained the plan of battle for the expulsion of the Russian forces from Ukraine and the restoration of order. Over the next six hours, Jefferson would limit his activity to absorbing as much of the enclosed information in these two folders as possible before his phone call with President Putin.

At 9:30, the President exited the Oval Office and walked down the hall to his Executive Secretary's office. There, sitting in a strait-backed wooden chair, was Tommy Hensley, his Russian interpreter on loan from the State Department. Jefferson extended his hand for a warm handshake and then invited Hensley to join him in the Oval Office. For the next twenty minutes, the two men discussed the tone the President wanted to take with Putin as well as some of the finer points of the current situation.

At 10:00PM, one of the phones on the President's desk rang and he picked up the handset. The operator told him that she had President Putin on the line and then put him through. Jefferson waited until he heard the definitive tone confirming the completion of the secure circuit and then began.

"President Putin, this is President Jefferson."

"Good evening, Mister President," came the response. "What may I do for you this chilly Winter morning?"

"You know damn well what you can do for me, Vladimir," blustered Jefferson. "Yesterday morning, before dawn, Russian troops invaded Ukraine at four points. Three elements headed for Kiev, Kharkiv, and Odessa, Ukraine's three largest cities. The fourth element headed for Kropyvnytskyi in central Ukraine, obviously to set up your command center for this invasion. Our satellites subsequently caught pictures of numerous Russian military aircraft on the tarmac at Kryvyi Rih International Airport 75 miles to the Southeast.

"It had been five years to the day since you re-annexed the Crimean peninsula. Your rationale then was that the majority of Crimea's residents were ethnic Russians. That may have been true. But the same cannot be said for the Ukrainian population as a whole. More than three-quarters of its population are ethnic Ukrainians and less than 20% are ethnic Russians.

"Here's what you are going to do. You will issue orders to your field commanders to withdraw from Kiev, Kharkiv, and Odessa by sundown tonight. They are to kill no Ukrainians except in self-defense and they are to damage no buildings or infrastructure. You will order your troops in central Ukraine to withdraw directly to the East and keep going until they are back on Russian soil. You will order your air force commander to have all his aircraft return to their home bases in Russia, also before sundown. Finally, you will have your warships of the Black Sea fleet return to their homeports as quickly as possible," he concluded.

"And why would I do such things?" asked Putin. "The Russian economy is far stronger than that of Ukraine. It is the ethnic Russians who contribute most to any economic or military strength which Ukraine may possess.

They were better off as a part of the Soviet Union and they will once again be better off as one of the Russian Federation of states."

"You and I both know that is not true, Vladimir," answered Jefferson, clearly losing his temper in spite of his interpreter's attempts at using the most temperate language he could while still conveying the content of the President's words. "Your economy is in shambles. And your military is no match for ours."

"Is that so?" asked Putin sarcastically. "Perhaps we will find out. My ground troops are now safely embedded in Ukraine's three largest cities. Any attempt to strike them from the air or by using ship-mounted guns or missiles will inevitably kill hundreds of civilians as well as damage numerous essential buildings and services. Our aircraft are in the geographic center of Ukraine. Your planes would have to travel hundreds of miles to strike them on the ground. If they were not shot down by SAM missiles, they would inevitably be overwhelmed by our superior aircraft."

"The only thing that is inevitable, Vladimir," Jefferson nearly shouted, "is that Ukraine is going to remain an independent nation. It's President, Petro Poroshenko, has stated that Ukraine will soon be a member of both the European Union and NATO.

"You have less than twelve hours for us to observe

irrefutable evidence that your troops are withdrawing and that your aircraft and warships are returning to their home bases and homeports respectively. If we do not observe such evidence, you, personally, will be held responsible for whatever the outcome is of any armed conflict.

"Are we clear, Mister President?" asked Jefferson in closing.

"Crystal, Mister Jefferson," replied Putin.

President Jefferson slammed down the phone. All President Putin could hear on the other end of the line was a click.

The President thanked his translator and dismissed him. Then he picked up the handset of another telephone and called General Milley at the National Military Command Center (NMCC), the so-called "war room", at the Pentagon. The NMCC is maintained by the Air Force and serves as the command and control center for the National Command Authority (NCA).

"General Milley, this is the President," began Jefferson. "I've just gotten off the phone with President Putin. He shows no sign of backing down on his intention to re-annex Ukraine. I gave him until sundown Kiev time to exhibit evidence that his troops, aircraft, and warships are withdrawing from the potential theater of battle. Should they do so, I'll want our intelligence community to keep both you, and me, informed. If not, I hereby authorize you to implement the battle plan with which you provided me this afternoon.

"There is, however, one issue which causes me grave concern. As with terrorists, the Russian troops with their tanks, guns, and SAM launchers have embedded themselves in the densely-populated neighborhoods of Ukraine's largest cities. They have also located our potential targets near key elements of those cities' infrastructures such as subway stations and power plants. I am sorely concerned that in the process of ridding the cities of the Russians we may do long-term damage to commerce and life as the Ukrainians currently know it."

"Leave that concern to me, Mister President," said General Milley. "I've got a surprise up my sleeve about which I doubt President Putin has any idea. All I'll need is a little help from your boys at Kessel Run up in Boston."

"Consider their total resources at your command for the duration of the hostilities," said Jefferson. "And tell General Goldfein of the Air Force I said to give you all needed assistance."

"Will do, Mister President," said Milley.

"Goodbye, General Milley," said the President.

100

Chapter Thirteen

Milley's first concern was to communicate the President's orders to his Joint Chiefs. He called Air Force General Goldfein, Navy Chief of Naval Operations Richardson, and Marine Commandant Neller and told each of them that the battle plan which they had jointly prepared for the President had been approved. If there was no definitive reconnaissance satellite evidence that the Russian troops, aircraft, and Black Sea fleet were withdrawing from their threatening positions by sundown Kiev time, they were each to commence their forces' segment of the plan.

The KH-13s orbit the earth roughly once every 90 minutes. And Russia had about 12 hours to show clear signs of their intentions to withdraw from Ukraine. That provided for 8 passes of a satellite. Since each orbit followed a slightly offset path, the coverage in the following 12 hours would cover the entire width of Ukraine twice during daylight hours, once between 6:00AM and Noon and once again between Noon and 6:00PM.

Air photo interpreters (PIs) would be able to compare the imagery from each first pass with that of the pass six hours later. The word on whether or not the latter images showed significant movement, and in the correct direction, would be forwarded up the chain of command in a matter of minutes. Based upon the PIs' findings, General Milley would inform the President of the Russians' actions and apparent intentions and the President would issue the appropriate order accordingly. Milley would then pass that order on to Goldfein, Richardson, and Neller.

In the meantime, there were two important phone calls which would have to be made. President Jefferson would have to call Ukrainian President Poroshenko and General Milley would have to find a means of making contact with Ukrainian Colonel General Serhiy Popko. What Jefferson would tell Poroshenko was straightforward. However, how he told him, as well as whether or not that information should be shared with others, was somewhat more problematic.

Ukraine was in the midst of a presidential campaign with the first round of voting scheduled to take place on March 31st. This resulted in a Continuity of Government (COG) dilemma. If Poroshenko were to be re-elected, everything would proceed apace. But there were 44 candidates for president. If one of the other 43 candidates received 50% plus one votes on March 31st, the entire agenda and plan of battle might have to be drastically altered based upon the new president's diplomatic agenda. If there were no clear winner, the second election among the highest vote-getters would occur on April 21st.

If a pro-Russian candidate were to be elected, it might well be the Americans who would end up withdrawing. If it was a pro-EU candidate, there could be days or weeks of consultation with the EU's 27 heads of state (the United Kingdom would tentatively be exiting the EU on March 29th) before any foreign policy decision could be reached. And if Poroshenko or someone else of a decidedly anti-Russian persuasion was elected, the military operations would proceed as planned.

It was now 11:00PM in Washington, 6:00AM in Kiev, if indeed that was where Poroshenko was. It took the White House switchboard nearly twenty minutes to track him down. He had taken refuge in a small safe house in Vinnytsia, a city 125 miles Southwest of Kiev. By 11:25, President Jefferson had Poroshenko on a secure line.

"Petro," said the President, "it's John Jefferson here. We've developed our battle plan to assist you. In the simplest of terms, fighter aircraft from Italy and bombers from Qatar will take out the Russian troops, their artillery, and the Russian aircraft on the ground in central Ukraine. They will be assisted by aircraft from one of our aircraft carriers headed for the Black Sea as well as the guns and guided missiles aboard the destroyers and cruisers accompanying her.

"We will be landing 2,000 Marines along the shoreline of the Black Sea to capture or eliminate any Russian troops or artillery which may have remained in Odessa. I expect there will be some airborne combat

103

between fighters as well as Russian attacks on our bombers. The technological superiority of our aircraft should be sufficient to carry the day. Our only concern would be any mobile SAM missile launchers which the Russians may have brought to their central Ukraine air operations center to protect their aircraft on the ground.

"Above the fray, flying in a figure-eight path with an East-West orientation to encompass all of Ukraine, will be a Boeing E-4 Advanced Airborne Command Post *Nightwatch* aircraft providing overwatch for the entire Ukrainian theater. Because it is capable of air-to-air refueling, it can stay on station for up to a full week. It would then be replaced by a duplicate aircraft while it flew back to an air base where it could undergo routine maintenance."

"You seem to have this all worked out," replied Poroshenko. "I appreciate the time and energy which you and your military staff have clearly put into the planning effort. But, as you know, I am in the midst of a presidential campaign. President Putin knows this all too well. My opponents, of which there are many, may attempt to use this conflict against me to bring into question my leadership skills."

"There's one sure way to guarantee that that does not happen," said Jefferson. "It is now February 28th in Kiev. Your elections do not take place until March 31st. By sundown your time this evening we should have a pretty clear indication as to whether or not Vladimir Putin intends to withdraw his troops, artillery, aircraft, and warships.

"If he does, you will be seen by your people as a leader who stood up to an aggressor who is a bully. If not, we will commence our attacks. I do not envision this as a protracted conflict. As with most battles which are essentially fought from and in the air, I do not expect it to last long. And I wouldn't be sending in the American military's best assets if I did not intend to win.

"Assuming the United States and Ukraine prevail over the Russian aggressors, you will be seen as a leader who was able to call upon your close ally, the Americans, in a time of crisis. By the time the elections take place, you may well be seen as a national hero. Your re-election will be virtually assured."

"I had not looked at it that way before," responded Poroshenko. "As bad as it seems now, it might be good for my campaign."

"And if, by some chance, you should lose the election," continued Jefferson, "your successor could be expected by the people to continue the policies which you have enacted. Either way, Ukraine remains a free and independent nation-state which has stood up to and stared down the bully Russian Federation. Even if you are no longer president, you will always be thought of as an invaluable counselor whose advice will be sought by your nation's leaders for decades to come," concluded Jefferson.

"I had never looked at it that way," said Poroshenko.

"Either way, both you and Ukraine win, Petro. One more thing. Right now my Chairman of the Joint Chiefs of Staff, our highest ranking military man, is speaking with your Colonel General Serhiy Popko. He is briefing him on our battle plan. Throughout the course of this conflict, tell him to call my General Milley if he should ever have any questions. He's a good man, and he's always available to be of service."

"I cannot thank you enough," said Poroshenko. "He will be one less person about whom I will have to worry, and he will be getting his information from a man who knows a whole lot more about war than do I."

"Let's keep in close contact over the next few days, Petro," said the President. "I need to hear from you personally how the battle is going *and* how your fellow Ukrainians are reacting. At the same time, I will keep you apprised if there are any changes in our plan of battle."

"I cannot thank you enough, Mister President," said Poroshenko. "And if all goes as I have outlined to our people, we will one day, hopefully soon, find ourselves fellow NATO allies. I will let you go now."

Chapter Fourteen

There were two issues which had the potential to disrupt or impede the prosecution of the American war effort in Ukraine. One was purely political and the other strictly military. The first was totally beyond the capacity of the United States to control while the second would be dropped in the lap of the staff at Kessel Run.

The first issue was the upcoming presidential election in Ukraine. It was possible that a cessation of the hostilities would occur before the March 31st elections. In that case, it was reasonable to expect that the outcome could be seen as having no impact upon the restoration of Ukrainian independence or its territorial integrity. But in geopolitics, nothing is for certain.

Among the 44 presidential candidates, there were only a handful of legitimate challengers to Poroshenko's regime. The opinion polls showed that he was not the statistical favorite at the time of the Russian invasion, but he nonetheless had a track record against which, for better or worse, his opponents would have to campaign.

The nation of Ukraine itself has one foot in Russia and the other in pro-Western Europe. Poroshenko had done his best to walk that tightrope while making it clear that he saw the nation's future tied to fostering alliances with and membership in both the European Union and NATO. Poroshenko believed that Ukraine's economic stability was contingent upon maintaining those alliances.

Poroshenko's election as president in 2014 and the strength of his campaign in 2019 was, in part, a result of the support of a pro-European movement, *Euromaidan* or "European Square", which arose in November of 2013 coupled with his apparent successful oversight of a number of economic reform programs. In 2015, the International Monetary Fund (IMF) gave Ukraine a $17.5 billion aid package and in 2018 supplemented that with a $3.9 billion line of credit. That line of credit, however, was extended contingent upon the implementation of a series of anti-corruption measures which placed some members of Poroshenko's administration at odds with those issuing the credit.

A Western financial analyst, Tim Ash, had said, "Poroshenko should not take Western support for granted . . . [He] will be called out for failings on the anti-corruption front and for failing to ensure free and fair elections."

But Continuity of Government in a nation so often embroiled in political turmoil is a major selling point, and Poroshenko had both represented and positioned himself as the sole candidate capable of providing that continuity if elected to a second term as president. His critics, however, had pictured him as having failed to carry out his promised anti-corruption measures while routinely antagonizing Ukraine's threatening neighbor, Russia.

One of Poroshenko's challengers was Yulia Tymoshenko, the leader of the "Fatherland" party. Her pro-European orientation and leadership of the "Orange Revolution" protests against corruption and electoral fraud in late 2004 had led to her viability as a presidential candidate. She had twice been prime minister, but she had also been the subject of various criminal investigations. She had been sentenced to seven years in prison in 2011, but the European human rights court subsequently ruled that both the charges and prison sentence had been politically motivated.

One of his most troubling challengers was Volodymyr Zelensky. He was a politician, screenwriter, and actor. In fact, he had once played the President of Ukraine in a television sitcom entitled "Servant of the People". The production company of the show subsequently created a party of the same name. Polling so well with the populace before he ever seriously contemplated running for the presidency, he ultimately announced his candidacy on New Year's Eve, 2018.

Among the second-tier candidates was Yuriy Boyko. He had served as both vice prime minister and fuel & energy minister. He was running as an independent candidate on a platform aligned with the center-left alliance Opposition

Platform – For Life. His greatest claim to fame was punching a fellow member of parliament in 2016 after being accused by him of being a "Kremlin agent".

Other second-tier candidates included Anatoliy Hrytsenko and Oleh Lyashko. While Hrytsenko was the leader of the Civil Position party and a former defense minister, Lyashko was a former journalist who now led the Radical Party. He had gone on a hunger strike in support of Tymoshenko when she was imprisoned.

The most recent polls had shown that the contest had been reduced to a "three-horse race" between Poroshenko, Tymoshenko, and Zelensky. Zelensky came in at 25 percent, followed by Poroshenko at 17 percent and Tymoshenko at 16 percent.

On March 4th, Teneo Intelligence reported, "Actor Volodymyr Zelensky has shot up in the polls ahead of the presidential election, while the campaign of the populist opposition leader Yulia Tymoshenko has begun to fade, impacting the probabilities of election scenarios. Zelensky is now the favorite to win the first round on 31 March, but a runoff on 21 April appears inevitable. He would likely win against Tymoshenko, but the odds for a potential runoff between Zelensky and incumbent President Petro Poroshenko appear level." They estimated that there was a 60 percent chance that Poroshenko would face Zelensky in a runoff in April.

The second issue which could potentially impede the American ability to prosecute the war in Ukraine was the availability of the weapon of choice to be loaded onto the F-15s, F-16s, F-18s, F-22s, and B-1Bs. To resolve this problem, the staff at Kessel Run would be working around the clock for the duration of the hostilities. But the app which they would be required to develop was in Kessel Run's wheelhouse and well within the lab's capability.

The secret weapon to which General Milley had alluded in his telephone discussion with President Jefferson was the BLU-129/B variant of the Mark 82 bomb. The Air Force had been ramping up the production of the air-dropped, precision-guided BLU-129/B bomb increasingly in demand by combat commanders – so accurate, lethal, and precise, it is called "the world's largest sniper accuracy".

In the 21st century, one of the greatest drawbacks to using bombs to conduct a war was the high incidence of the threat of injury or death to non-combatants and the collateral damage to surrounding buildings and infrastructure. As a result, the BLU-129/B, also known as the Very Low Collateral Damage Weapon or VLCDW, was developed to respond to that concern. But, with the finite quantity of VLCDWs available, the key to driving back the Russians to within their own borders was to have the appropriate weapon available to mount onto the aircraft flying from Aviano, Al Udeid, Incirlik, and the *Truman*.

The VLCDWs markedly differ from the standard 500-pound warheads housed in the Mark 82 bomb. They are adaptable carbon fiber warheads engineered specifically to limit the "field effects" of detonation. According to Captain Hope Cronin, a military spokeswoman, "The Air Force is currently producing BLU-129 bomb bodies to address operational demand."

There are two unique aspects to the BLU-129/B. The first is that the housing of the warhead is carbon fiber instead of steel. Upon detonation, a steel bomb disperses shrapnel in all directions injuring or killing persons as well as inflicting heavy damage on buildings and associated facilities. When the BLU-129/B detonates, the carbon fiber vaporizes, thereby creating no flying debris and severely limiting the "blast radius". That means that using today's laser-guided bombs and more precise targeting technologies, the bomb can more accurately strike where it is aimed and destroy such targets as artillery, tanks, and aircraft without injuring civilians or enemy combatants. And an enemy combatant without their tank or aircraft can reasonably be expected to flee the scene.

The second unique quality of the BLU-129/B is that, as intelligence about the targets is relayed to the pilot in real time, they can instantaneously adjust the blast power of the detonation while in flight en route to those targets. Consequently, they can limit the power of the blast to only that necessary to destroy the target while minimizing or eliminating the loss of life. The value of these weapons in fighting the war against the Russians in Ukraine cannot be overstated.

The BLU-129/B warheads represent a feat of engineering and materials science which was reached by the Air Force working in collaboration with the Lawrence Livermore National Laboratory (LLNL), a research center of the Department of Energy well known for its work in developing atomic bombs.

The engineers at LLNL use a special machine to wrap carbon fiber filament to produce the housings for the BLU-129/B. It was essential that the carbon fiber housing be rugged enough to withstand the forces exerted upon it while flying attached to a supersonic aircraft or falling thousands, if not tens of thousands, of feet while still producing no fragments when the warhead was detonated. The development, which began in 2010, was facilitated by the use of supercomputer-generated models and simulations to determine how the bomb's housing would react to these various stresses. According to an article in the March 2013 issue of the LLNL's internal *Science & Technology Review* magazine, scientists and engineers did 95 percent of the design work through modeling rather than physical testing and prototyping.

According to LLNL's project manager, Kip Hamilton,

"In the 'old' days, we would build a prototype, test it, and revamp it based on the results. Our advanced modeling and simulation capabilities reduce the time needed to determine the final design specifications for munitions." It was also said that LLNL designed the warhead's prototype to lend itself to mass production. But, at a cost of $116,000 per warhead, such streamlined production has still not taken place.

According to Colonel Gary Haase of the Air Force Research Laboratory (AFRL), "There are limited numbers of this weapon, and we want to hold onto it for those missions which need to have only that capability. We want to have options and flexibility so we can take out this one person with a hit-to-kill munition, or crank it up and take out a truck or a wide area." The warheads are manufactured by Aerojet Rocketdyne in El Segundo, California, a city made famous as the home to the Douglas Aircraft Company during and after World War II.

Aerojet Rocketdyne has stated, "These weapons use carbon-fiber-wound construction of the warhead casing. . . A carbon-fiber-wound bomb body disintegrates instead of fragmenting, which adds explosive force nearby, but lowers collateral damage." Colonel Haase added, the BLU-129/B's "multi-mode energetics" permit the pilot to leverage its advanced "smart fuse" technology to adjust the blast effect.

Such flexibility which allows the pilot to adjust a

warhead's destructive characteristics while in flight provides new options when strategizing Concepts of Operations (CONOPS). The ability to alter a munition's characteristics on the fly, as it were, will alter the types of attack missions falling within the realm of possibility. In 2013, Skip Hamilton said, "The way wars are fought now is vastly different than it was even 15 years ago. More consideration is given to protecting warfighters in close proximity to targets and to civilians not engaged in the fight."

In terms of the war in Ukraine, the F-15 *Eagles* could carry 11 BLU-129/Bs, the F-16 *Fighting Falcons* 9, the F-18 *Super Hornets* 9, and the F-22 *Raptors* 10. But each hardpoint used for a BLU-129/B meant one less air-to-air missile which might be needed for aerial combat or air-to-surface missile to strike a moving target on the ground. However, the B-1B *Lancer* put them all to shame with its capacity to carry 84 BLU-129/B warheads in the general purpose Mark 82 bomb housings.

Back in Boston at the Kessel Run Experimentation Lab, several teams of engineers and coders were working on an app which could be distributed by means of the Air Force's classified network to the air operations centers at Aviano, Al Udeid, and Incirlik, as well as to the munitions team aboard the USS *Harry S. Truman*. Its purpose would be straightforward. It would determine the number of BLU-129/B warheads which were needed daily at each of the four air operations launch sites and ensure that the requisite number was not only available but on site before each day's missions were launched.

There were a number of variables which would have to be plugged into the app each day to get the necessary numbers. The first, and most obvious, was the number of targets to be struck daily which would require a VLCDW. The second was the numerical designator for each of the four launch sites. The third was the number and availability of different aircraft capable of transporting bombs to those launch sites as well as their locations at any given time. And, fourth, the rate at which the factory producing the BLU-129/Bs in El Segundo could get them to the closest Air Force base for transport. Ironically, Los Angeles Air Force Base was located in El Segundo, but, as a facility of the Air Force Space Command, it was a non-flying base. The closest base with an airfield capable of handling large transports turned out to be March Air Force Base in Riverside, home to the Air Force's 452nd Air Mobility Wing with its fleet of C-17 *Globemaster IIIs*, the most agile of the Air Force's jet transports.

So now the task fell to Kessel Run to develop an app, working 24/7, to establish a pipeline to get those 129s from El Segundo via the *Globemaster IIIs* at March to Aviano, Al Udeid, and Incirlik, as well as onto the deck of the *Truman* via Naval Air Station Sigonella in Sicily using their C-2A(R) twin-turboprop *Greyhound* cargo aircraft capable of carrying twenty 129s each flight. It would be codenamed SNIPER.

Chapter Fifteen

On the morning of Thursday, February 28th, in Moscow, when President Jefferson called Vladimir Putin to tell him that he had until sundown that day to exhibit his nation's military forces withdrawing from Ukraine or else the American military would take action, he was bluffing. Yes, there were military aircraft in Italy, Qatar, and Turkey which could easily strike Russian targets within Ukraine, but they did not yet have in the air bases' ammunition bunkers the ordnance desired to conduct those strikes. Moreover, the USS *Harry S. Truman* was still en route from Naples to the Black Sea. The earliest the United States could launch the offensive it had planned would not come until sunrise on Sunday, March 3rd.

President Putin, of course, had no way of knowing this. Nonetheless, he had immediately called a meeting of his top military advisors to be convened in the main conference room in the Kremlin for Noon that day. The agenda consisted of a single question; was Ukraine worth the risk of engaging in a shooting war with the United States? The outcome of that meeting would dictate if the troops, heavy artillery, and aircraft would be withdrawn from Ukraine or not.

At 11:45AM, the line of black Aurus Senat limousines pulling up to the main administrative entrance to the

Kremlin stretched all the way to the arched entryway to the inner courtyard of the Kremlin itself. The temperature in Moscow was still well below freezing, and each limo's occupant exited his vehicle garbed in his heavy wool dress topcoat with the insignia of his rank prominently displayed upon his epaulets. Not a single attendee's uniform displayed fewer than two stars except for the General of the Army, the Admiral of the Fleet, the Marshal of Aviation, and the Marshal of the Russian Federation himself, each of whose shoulder boards was emblazoned with a single oversized star which extended its full width.

Each of these senior officers made a grand entrance, walking up the stairs and passing through the main doors of the administrative wing of the Kremlin which were being held open by senior non-commissioned officers. They then each walked the long hallways of the Kremlin to the conference room where they took their seats in rank order with the chair at the head of the ornate conference table reserved for the Russian President. Only when all else were seated did Vladimir Putin enter the room from the adjacent sitting room accompanied by his Foreign Minister, Sergey Lavrov.

"Good morning, Gentlemen," began Putin. "The troops under each of your commands have done an enviable job reaching their destinations within Ukraine. For that I congratulate you.

"Six hours ago, the President of the United States called me and issued an ultimatum. If our troops, heavy artillery, warships, and aircraft do not exhibit their intent to withdraw from Ukraine by sundown today, the American military will have no other choice than to come to the aid of Ukraine to repel or destroy our military assets within their borders. I want to hear from the heads of each of our services, and then I will ask our Marshal of the Russian Federation to summarize your remarks and make his recommendation. General Shoygu, let us begin with you."

Sergey Shoygu, General of the Army, cleared his throat and began.

"Mister President, our ground troops on all four fronts have made excellent progress. They have set up their command headquarters in the city of Kropyvnytskyi in central Ukraine. Troops from the North have occupied Kiev and control most parts of the city. Moreover, they have embedded themselves, their tanks, and their artillery in areas which are either densely populated or surrounded by critical industrial complexes or vital infrastructure facilities like factories, power plants, or subway stations. The Americans would not dare bomb these targets as to do so would kill many innocent civilians as well as destroy the sources of their economic vitality.

"In Kharkiv, the situation is the same. Only there, the troops and equipment are now entrenched adjacent to historic religious landmarks as well. Their destruction would not only enrage the natives but also evoke an outcry from the American population as a whole. Finally, our troops which entered Ukraine from Crimea and established themselves in Odessa met with little to no resistance. They have set up tanks along the perimeter of the Ukrainian Navy installation there to prevent a breakout by the sailors. And, as in the cases of both Kiev and Kharkiv, they have ringed the city with their mobile SAM launchers to prevent an incursion by enemy aircraft," he concluded.

"Very good, Sergey. Very good indeed," said Putin. "Now on to you, General Yudin."

"Things are going very well with the Air Force," said Andrey Yudin, Marshal of Aviation. "We have occupied what is known as Kryvyi Rih International Airport 75 miles Southeast of Kropyvnytskyi. The Army has lent us a number of their mobile SAM launchers which we have deployed around the airfield to protect the aircraft on the ground which we have flown in from bases throughout Russia.

"We now have multiple squadrons of both MiG-31 supersonic interceptors and Su-57 stealth supersonic jet fighters on the ground. We plan on using the MiGs to enforce a no-fly zone above Ukraine while the '57s will attack any enemy aircraft which should evade our perimeter. Both aircraft are equipped with rotary cannons and air-to-air missiles. The '57 is capable of Mach 2 while the MiG can reach Mach 2.8. Between these two aircraft, we should be able to control the skies and protect our assets on the ground. We saw no need to bring in any of our Tu-23 or Tu-160 bombers as we do not expect any enemy targets on the ground."

"Well done, Andrey," said Putin in response to the report. "It sounds as though you and your senior staff have thought this through well. Finally, Admiral Korolyov, how goes it with our Black Sea Fleet?" Vladimir Korolyov was Admiral of the Fleet, the top naval officer in the Russian Federation.

"Sir," began the admiral, "we view this as a conflict where most of the combat, if any, will take place in the air. We have designed our strategy to ensure that no enemy warships can get within range of Ukraine's Southern coastline and hit our land-based assets with their guns. What we have essentially done is created a cordon made up of cruisers, destroyers, and frigates beyond the capability of enemy artillery to strike inland. I do not envision any armed conflict will take place in the Black Sea itself."

"I see," observed President Putin. "Thank you, Vladimir. Now, Marshal Sergeyev, your conclusions please." Igor Sergeyev was the Marshal of the Russian Federation, the highest ranking military officer in the entire nation.

"Mister President," responded Sergeyev, "these three officers have done their jobs admirably. The Army successfully breached the Ukrainian border and each unit made it to their intended destination. They have embedded themselves at crucial locations in Ukraine's three largest cities; Kiev, Kharkiv, and Odessa. They have also established a command and control center in central Ukraine.

"As for the Air Force, they have commandeered an airfield in central Ukraine from which they can enforce a no-fly zone with their MiG interceptors while being prepared to shoot down any enemy fighter or bomber with their '57s. Finally, the Navy will secure the Black Sea coastline so that no enemy ships will be able to fire their guns to reach land while, at the same time, no enemy troops can come ashore should they wish to engage in a land battle.

"I approved this three-pronged approach, and they have executed it as ordered. I envision this campaign not as much a war of attrition of soldiers or equipment as attrition of will. The Ukrainians do not possess the troops or hardware to stand up to our ground or air forces. Our men and machines are already part of the landscape of their three major centers of population.

"Our troops will ultimately be seen not so much as combatants as occupiers. We will continue to supplement their numbers while rotating those who have served the longest in Ukraine back home so that our men on the ground do not become complacent. In the end, Poroshenko, or whoever succeeds him, will simply have to give in to the inevitability of Ukraine once again being integrated back into the Russian Federation where their lives will be less contentious while our resources and their warm water ports will enhance their economy as well as our own.

"As for the ultimatum issued by the American President, we should have expected nothing less. But the American people have a finite tolerance for warfare. They have been at war since 1991. First, it was with Hussein, initially in Kuwait and subsequently in Iraq. Then, following in the same disastrous path as Russia itself, it was with the Taliban in Afghanistan. And, finally, it was with ISIS in both Syria *and* Iraq, as well as in Northern Africa.

"The Americans have become weary of bloodshed, both abroad and at home. In addition to overseas wars in which many questioned whether their own country had any vested interest, they are now dealing with terrorist cells within their own borders. The multiple coordinated terrorist attacks in New York City's Times Square brought the war with ISIS onto American soil. They no longer have the stomach for it. Much as was the sentiment in the United States in the latter years of the Vietnam War, the prevailing sentiment became to declare victory and bring the boys home.

"Ultimately they did so in Vietnam, and they will soon do the same with ISIS in Syria. And neither Vietnam nor ISIS was envisioned as the military dreadnought which we are portrayed as being by their think tanks or in their press. You have asked me for my opinion. That opinion is that we stay right where we are, wear down the resistance of the Ukrainian people, and characterize Ukraine as nothing more than a rogue republic which will be re-integrated into the Russian Federation."

"Thank you, Marshal Sergeyev," concluded President Putin. "I think I have heard enough. It seems that we hold the upper hand on the ground, in the air, and at sea. If we were to relent in this endeavor now, Ukraine would persevere in its attempts at becoming an integral part of the EU, NATO, and Europe. This we cannot allow.

"I am going to call President Jefferson's bluff. We will leave our troops in Ukraine and augment them over time until they become nothing more than part of the scenery. We will maintain our aircraft in central Ukraine and ensure that a finite number is always on alert should the unexpected occur. And we will keep the warships of our Black Sea Fleet in a cordon off the Southern coast in the event of an enemy offensive.

"I will not dignify President Jefferson's threat with either a phone call or press release. We will simply remain."

Chapter Sixteen

Ever since President Jefferson contacted General Milley on the evening of February 26th, the imagery analysts at the Air Force's 24th Intelligence Squadron at Ramstein Air Base in Germany had been carefully scrutinizing the photos of Ukraine coming in from all the intelligence, surveillance, and reconnaissance (ISR) platforms at their disposal including the KH-13 *Misty* satellites, the Northrop Grumman RQ-4 *Global Hawk* reconnaissance drones, and high-altitude stealth aircraft equipped with side-looking airborne radar (SLAR). Other sources included *Predator* and *Reaper* drones as well as manned aircraft such as the U-2 *Dragon Lady* spy plane, the RC-135 *Rivet Joint*, and the MC-12 *Liberty*.

The images from these surveillance platforms a thousand miles or more away were bounced off orbiting satellites and received in near real-time at Ramstein. Analysts in a dimly-lit room sat staring at their computer screens, capturing images and reporting summaries of their observations to their superior officers. Those officers consolidated their cumulative intelligence findings and transmitted them securely to the commanding officer of the Air Combat Command (ACC), formerly the Tactical Air Command, General James Holmes at ACC headquarters at Langley Air Force Base, Virginia. After reviewing the intelligence take from Germany, Holmes securely transmitted the findings, along with his recommendations, to General Goldfein, the Air Force Chief of Staff, at the Pentagon.

On Saturday morning, General Goldfein sat down in General Milley's conference room with the Naval CNO, the Marine Corps Commandant, the Army Chief of Staff, and the Chairman of the Joint Chiefs. As could have been predicted, his report indicated that there was literally no movement on the part of the Russians to withdraw from Ukraine. The Army had deeply embedded itself in its three largest cities where they had concluded that the damage to the civilian population, infrastructure, and economy inflicted by American bombs would be the greatest. The Air Force had brought squadrons of MiG-31 and Su-57 fighters into an airfield in central Ukraine and was now attempting to enforce a no-fly zone over the entire nation. Finally, the Navy's Black Sea Fleet had cordoned off the Southern coastline at a distance from shore which would prevent the shelling of land-based targets from any enemy warship.

It was concluded that the battle plan originally envisioned on the day Russia invaded Ukraine would still be the most effective one. The aircraft at Aviano and Al Udeid had been serviced and were prepared to function at their peak performance levels. President Erdoğan in Turkey was still allowing American aircraft to take off from Incirlik. And Carrier Strike Group 8 with the USS *Harry S. Truman* as its flagship would be in the heart of the Black Sea by

Sunday morning.

There were only two components of the plan which were not yet fully fleshed out, but both were being worked on. The first was the landing of the 2,000 Marines of the Marine expeditionary unit, Task Force 62, on the coast East and West of Odessa. The strike group could try to create a diversion allowing the *Mount Whitney* to breach the cordon or it could simply penetrate the cordon by force. Clearly, the first option was preferable.

The second component still up in the air, literally, was the availability of a sufficient supply of BLU-129/Bs to provide for the adequate arming of all the fighter aircraft and bombers which would be striking soft targets in the first sorties of the operation on Sunday morning. Aerojet Rocketdyne was cranking them out 24 hours a day, and the *Globemaster IIIs* from March were ferrying them to the three air bases and one naval air station which was forwarding them on to the *Truman*. The fleet of C-17s was keeping the KC-135 *Stratotankers* from the 100th ARW in the air for refueling around the clock.

Back at Kessel Run in Boston, those segments of SNIPER which would enable the Air Force to keep those fighters and bombers supplied with VLCDWs which had been completed and tested had been distributed to the air operations centers via the Air Force's secure network. But those components only served to establish the "conveyor belt" between El Segundo and the theater of operations. The more intricate task was that of knowing, ahead of time, how many BLU-129/Bs were needed each at Aviano, Al Udeid, Incirlik, and aboard the *Truman*. And *that* task was in turn dependent upon the reports coming out of the 24th Intelligence Squadron at Ramstein and making their way first to Langley and then the Pentagon. Ultimately, someone had to take the risk of upsetting the chain of command. And that someone was *Captain* Bryon Kroger.

At dawn on Thursday morning, roughly 65 hours before the first sorties were scheduled to take off for Ukraine, Kroger had picked up a secure line and called the National Military Command Center at the Pentagon. He told the watch officer that it was imperative that he speak to General Milley, Chairman of the Joint Chiefs. The watch officer was Air Force Captain Michael Jensen who held the same rank as Kroger.

"By what authority are you making this request?" asked Jensen.

"On my own authority as the Chief Operating Officer of the Kessel Run Experimentation Lab in Boston. Listen, *Captain*," proceeded an irritated Bryon Kroger, "If you don't put me through to General Milley immediately, you may well be responsible for the deaths of thousands of Ukrainians and possibly hundreds of our own servicemen. Now, do you want to accept that responsibility, or are you going to put me through?"

Captain Jensen knew that the Russians had invaded Ukraine earlier in the week, and he knew that the American military was gearing up to come to the aid of the Ukrainians. He'd never heard of Kessel Run, but this guy on the phone seemed to know what he was talking about. All Jensen really cared about was getting one more good Officer Performance Report so that he could make the "Major" eligibility list.

"Putting you through, Captain Kroger," was all he said.

The secure line in the Chairman's residence at Fort Myer rang. He picked it up on the first ring.

"What time is it?" were the first words out of his mouth.

"6:27AM, Sir," said Kroger.

"Who the Hell *is* this?" asked Milley.

"Captain Bryon Kroger, Sir," responded the captain. "Chief Operating Officer of Kessel Run Experimentation Lab in Boston." Now he had Milley's full attention.

"What can I do for you, Captain?" asked Milley.

"We're less than 72 hours away from a major air assault on Russian forces in Ukraine. My staff has been working around the clock to make sure that the aircraft staging that assault are loaded with the appropriate ordnance. But the intelligence which will dictate what will get struck and with what variant of warhead is coming out of the 24th at Ramstein.

"Right now, that intelligence has to pass through both ACC headquarters at Langley and the office of the Chief of Staff of the Air Force before I receive it. Depending upon those two senior officers' schedules, I'm getting it hours after it becomes available. I'm asking that you cut through the red tape ASAP so that I see the take from Ramstein as soon as, if not before, General Holmes gets it at Langley. Only then will my engineers and coders be able to get their job completed by the time the ordnance is onloaded onto the aircraft for their sunrise sorties on Sunday."

"It doesn't take a lot for a junior officer to get me pissed off at 6:27AM, Captain," said Milley, "but I have to give you credit for putting it all on the line in the best interests of the Air Force and the country. I'll call General August at Ramstein as soon as you hang up and I have a chance to take a leak. I'll have him get on to the commander at the 24th and instruct him to loop you in on all intelligence relative to the Ukraine operation as soon as, if not before, it goes to General Holmes at Langley. They write nice little summaries for Jim, but all you're asking for is the raw intel and the nature and location of the targets selected. From that, you'll be able to tell your engineers and coders just what they need to do their jobs. No elaboration."

"Thank you very much, Sir," replied Kroger. "We'll get the AOCs everything they need before they need it. That's a promise."

I'll hold you to it," said Milley in closing. "Good day."

Chris Knowles

Chapter Seventeen

Those components of SNIPER which were not yet completed by the staff at Kessel Run were geared to assisting the Aviation Ordnance Loaders (AOLs) at Aviano, Al Udeid, Incirlik, and aboard the *Truman* perform their tasks to maximize the effect of the weapons loaded on each aircraft. For the AOLs, it was not only the mix of weapons with which each aircraft was armed but, in the case of the B-1B *Lancers*, the order in which those weapons were loaded. The evidence of that would become clear on Sunday morning.

By Noon on February 28th, Kessel Run's secure network link was downloading images from the 24th Intelligence Squadron at Ramstein with red grease pencil circles around the targets for Sunday's assault. Moreover, in the margin of each photograph was an annotation giving not only the number of Mark 82 bombs with which each target was to be struck but the variant of warhead with which each bomb was to be armed. It was those annotations which the final components of SNIPER would process and with which Kessel Run's engineers and coders would ensure that the Aviation Ordnance Loaders were directed to appropriately arm each aircraft.

Using that portion of SNIPER which maintained the conveyor belt of C-17s between March Air Force Base and the theater of operations, the app would now guarantee that the supply of BLU-129/B warheads was distributed in such a way that each aircraft would get their required allotment of those warheads in theater. It would be the responsibility of the AOL to keep track of the supply of other warheads which might be needed as well as the number of air-to-air and air-to-surface missiles required to be mounted on each of the fighter's hardpoints. Fighting an air war over Ukraine with warheads being built in California was akin to Napoleon's capturing Moscow during the War of 1812 and then suffering defeat, not at the hands of the Russian army but due to his army's demand for sustenance and supplies which could not be fulfilled by supply lines stretching back as far as from Smolensk to Paris.

With the raw intel from the 24th IS and production numbers from Aerojet Rocketdyne as source variables, SNIPER was putting the correct mix of warheads on the tarmac at the airfields and on the deck of the *Truman* on the Black Sea. As zero hour approached for the aircraft's pre-dawn takeoffs for Ukrainian airspace, the AOLs had all their respective ordnance onloaded. For the fighters, the mix of Mark 82s and missiles was based upon the level of resistance which the squadron commanders had been led to believe their aircraft would encounter. For the B-1B *Lancers* at Al Udeid, the problem was somewhat different.

The *Lancer's* capacity to carry 84 Mark 82 bombs made it an invaluable weapon in and of itself. But loaded in such a manner, it had no means of defense. Well before it reached Ukrainian airspace, each *Lancer* would have to have picked up fighter aircraft escorts to ensure its safety. Of course, each *Lancer* had a sophisticated suite of Electronic Countermeasures (ECMs) built into its avionics systems, but they only slowed down attacking enemy fighters; they did not destroy them. That task would be left to the American fighter escort.

The battle plan drawn up by the Joint Chiefs called for 36 of the 42 F-16 *Fighting Falcons* from the 510th and 555th at Aviano to participate in the assault. Seven each would head for Kiev, Kharkiv, Odessa, and Kropyvnytskyi. The F-16 could carry a combination of 2 air-to-air missiles and 9 Mark 82s or trade off 2 Mark 82s each for another pair of missiles. The decision was made to arm each of those 28 aircraft with 4 AIM-9 *Sidewinder* air-to-air missiles and 7 Mark 82s carrying BLU-129/B warheads. The remaining eight *Fighting Falcons* would fly the length of the Black Sea South of the Ukrainian territorial waters and rendezvous with the two *Lancers* flying North from Qatar.

Any available F-22 *Raptors* at Incirlik would fly North from Turkey to join the *Lancer* formations. They would each exclusively carry 6 AIM-120 Advanced Medium-Range Air-to-Air (AMRAAM) missiles to supplement their 6-barrel rotary cannons. Along with the *Fighting Falcons*, the *Raptors* would fly escort for the vulnerable B-1B *Lancers*. The two *Lancers* each had one primary target and two secondary targets.

That primary target was the same for both *Lancers*; the Russian aircraft on the ground at the Kryvyi Rih International Airport Southeast of Kropyvnytskyi. They had each been loaded with 12 GBU-31 Joint Direct Attack Munition (JDAM) GPS-guided bombs and 42 Mark 82 BLU-129/B VLCDW warheads. The secret of the effectiveness of their strike on the airfield lay with the Aviation Ordnance Loaders. The Mark 82s were loaded first followed by the JDAMs. Thus, when the *Lancers* reached the airfield, the dozen JDAMs could be released on the aircraft on the ground while retaining the VLCDWs for their secondary targets. The AOLs had followed a business model of inventory control which MBAs are taught in graduate school; last in-first out, or LIFO.

The secondary targets for the *Lancers* were mutually exclusive. One would hit Russian Army forces and hardware embedded in Kiev and Kharkiv with their 42 VLCDWs, all the while escorted and defended by four *Fighting Falcons* and half of the available *Raptors*. The second *Lancer* would strike Russian Army encampments in Kropyvnytskyi and Odessa. It would likewise be accompanied by four *Fighting Falcons* and the remaining *Raptors*.

Fresh to the fight would be two flights each of F-18 *Super Hornets* off the deck of the *Truman* carrying 9 Mark

82s each armed with BLU-129/Bs flying in the wake of the *Lancers* in an attempt to hit targets missed by the F-16s and B-1Bs.

By the end of the day on Friday, March 1st, all was in readiness. Routes had been worked out and inflection points in the aircraft's courses had been programmed into the flight computers. The pilots had all met with their commanders and been given the "big picture" view of the conflict. The final flight briefings would take place at between 4:00 and 5:00AM local time on Sunday morning.

Saturday was set aside for some downtime for the pilots before their combat missions. They had all been flying combat drills for the past 48 hours. Be it in the Ward Room aboard the *Truman* or in pilot lounges in Italy and Qatar, pilots were stretched out on couches or cots watching first-run films or episodes of the most popular TV shows which had been released on DVDs.

The meals the aircrews were being fed were a cut above those served to the average airman or sailor and were formulated by a nutritionist to not create discomfort during hours-long missions which, for most, would require one or more air-to-air refuelings. Pilots are prima donnas, each with his own set of quirks and eccentricities. The military looked the other way because warfare in the 21st century required their unique skill set.

All the pilots were gently awakened on Sunday morning. Those who preferred, showered and shaved before donning their flight suits. After a light breakfast and a cup of strong coffee, the pilots assembled in their respective briefing rooms. They were provided with their air target charts which had been generated at Ramstein as well as shown the latest imagery of their targets. Both their commanders and their units' intelligence officers were available for any last minute questions.

When the last inquiry had been answered to the pilot's satisfaction, it was time to saddle up. The pilots and, where appropriate, their Range Intercept Officers (RIOs) climbed the ladders of their aircraft and strapped themselves into their cockpits. At their airfields, the *Fighting Falcons* and *Lancers* followed the directions from their control towers and were airborne before the sun began to break the horizon. Aboard the *Truman*, the Commander, Air Group (CAG) gave the orders to his men on the deck and the aircraft took off one by one toward the West into the dark with the rising sun on their "six o'clock".

Russian MiG-31s enforcing the Southern perimeter of the no-fly zone were the first to become aware of the American assault. They immediately notified their superiors who passed the word on up the chain of command. At roughly 7:30AM on the morning of Sunday, March 3rd, Russian President Vladimir Putin was informed that the Russian military assets in Ukraine were under attack.

Chapter Eighteen

The first bombs to rain down on Ukraine were the 24 JDAM warheads dropped by the two escorted B-1B *Lancers*. They fell onto Kryvyi Rih International Airport. This was by design and for three specific reasons.

First, all of the MiG-31 supersonic interceptors which were not currently patrolling the no-fly zone were on the ground there, either for maintenance or awaiting the call to relieve one of the MiGs currently in the air. Secondly, all of the Su-57 supersonic fighters were parked there awaiting a possible enemy attack somewhere in Ukraine. And, finally, in addition to destroying the aircraft on the ground, the explosions would leave the single North – South runway full of gaps in the concrete and consequently unusable for either takeoffs or landings by the Russian Air Force aircraft. This meant that the Su-57 supersonic fighters among the aircraft on the airfield, even if they had been left airworthy by the terrible conflagration on the ground, could not be scrambled to pursue the American aircraft.

From there, one of the B-1Bs with their escort headed first for Kiev and then Kharkiv while the other flew 75 miles to the Northwest to Kropyvnytskyi and then South to Odessa. At their destinations, each of the *Lancers* and their accompanying *Flying Falcons* would drop half of their BLU-129/Bs. Only the *Raptors* would hold their launch of

139

AIM-120 AMRAAMs unless attacked by Russian fighters.

Their arrivals at Kiev, Kharkiv, Kropyvnytskyi, and Odessa followed right on the tail of the initial bomb attacks by the first wave of F-16s from Aviano and shortly before the cleanup F-18 *Super Hornets* from the *Truman*. At the end of the three waves of bombings with the VLCDWs, most of the Russian military targets had been destroyed while there was little to no damage to the surrounding buildings or structures and their occupants. What nominal damage had been done could not compare to that which the Russian Army had inflicted, or could inflict, upon the population and the metropolises if they so desired. Kessel Run had done its job admirably.

As for the American aircraft returning to their bases or aircraft carrier, none sustained significant damage though several had been pursued by the MiG-31s enforcing the no-fly zone and been hit by the stray round from their GSh-6-23 23mm rotary cannons before they reached international airspace. None of the damage affected their airworthiness, but most were in need of air-to-air refueling from either the 100th ARW or the 340th EARS. Only the *Super Hornets* made it back to the *Truman* on their initial tank of fuel.

No sooner had the attacking aircraft exited the theater of operations than the ISR platforms gone to work assessing the damage inflicted upon the Russian Army and Air Force equipment on the ground. Both daylight and infrared images were accumulated for all of the day's targets and transmitted to the 24th IS at Ramstein. The imagery analysts in Germany could assess the level of destruction achieved from the black & white daylight images and the infrared images would clearly show what was still burning.

Considering that the VLCDWs are unguided bombs, the 78% destruction rate of the targeted Russian assets was extraordinary. Only the JDAMs dropped on the airfield were GPS-guided. There, although only about 65% of the aircraft had been irreparably damaged, the loss of the airfield not only removed the potential effectiveness of the remaining 35% had they been able to take off but they could neither be flown back to their home bases for repairs nor replacement aircraft flown back in until the runway had been adequately repaired.

In Moscow, President Putin and the senior military leadership were receiving reports from across Ukraine. Marshal of the Russian Federation Igor Sergeyev had personally endorsed the tactics for the assault on Ukraine. And President Putin had himself approved it. Now they were in the position of having to formulate a Plan B if such a plan even existed. Even though, in reality, Plan A had been defeated by the American military, all the man on the street would care about was that Russia had tried, by force, to bring Ukraine back into the fold and failed.

In Washington there was jubilation. President

Jefferson had called a meeting of the Joint Chiefs for Sunday afternoon in the Situation Room. When they convened, the President congratulated the group collectively and then, with the exception of Marine Commandant Neller, each of them personally. The Marine expeditionary unit had not yet been called upon to subdue Odessa. But the fight was not over.

The senior military men were all for going back in on Monday morning and finishing off the job. But they were warriors. President Jefferson, though a hawk unlike his predecessor, the dovish Terrence Hayes, was a politician and had other ideas. He was going to give Vladimir Putin 48 hours to think over what had just transpired and give him a second chance to withdraw before 100% of his military assets were destroyed and a significant portion of Russia's young fighting men was killed in what was clearly a failed effort at the re-annexation of Ukraine.

There was vocal resistance from all parties of the Joint Chiefs. Each pointed out in their own way that to do so would give Putin the opportunity to bring in reinforcements. Moreover, the element of surprise would be lost. But the diplomatic element to Jefferson's approach would earn him much political capital, both abroad and at home. And another day, in another military conflict, he might need that capital to assure that his agenda was carried out.

He told the assembled group that he was going to get President Putin on the phone again. This time he would point out the losses which Russia had suffered and offer him the opportunity to avoid any further loss of life or materiel by withdrawing back within Russia's boundaries. If the Russian forces were observed to be heading back home, America would hold its fire. If not, the second round of attacks would be devised to result in the total annihilation of the Russian offensive force, both mechanical and human. The Joint Chiefs reluctantly conceded.

As soon as the meeting broke up, he directed his Chief of Staff to schedule another phone call with Putin, this one to take place at 6:00PM Washington time, 2:00AM on Monday morning Moscow time. He also told the Chief of Staff to have his interpreter from the State Department available no later than 5:30. He would once again place the call from the Oval Office. President Jefferson would now take time to collect his thoughts and formulate his approach.

At 6:00PM, President Jefferson was put through to President Putin in Moscow.

"Good morning, Vladimir," began Jefferson. "I'm very sorry that you did not accept the offer which I extended you previously. Russian tanks, aircraft, and lives could have been saved if only you had ordered your commanders to withdraw from Ukraine."

"I had no intention of accepting your offer, Mister Jefferson, and, for your information, it is not morning but the middle of the night here," said Putin sarcastically. "Ukraine has always been an integral part of the Russian Empire. When we became the Soviet Union, it was an essential republic of the USSR. There are many Russian loyalists in Ukraine who would like nothing more than to come home. Why would you believe I would betray them?"

"The dissolution of the Soviet Union created Ukraine as a sovereign nation," replied Jefferson. "They have a right to defend themselves, even from you. Your need for warm water ports and your desire to expand the territorial holdings of the Russian Federation at the expense of both Europe and the Ukrainians are not excuses for invading and occupying a sovereign state. But I know that your economy is in dire straits and that you must put forward a strong front to maintain the loyalty of your citizens to both you and the Russian Federation.

"I am going to give you a second, and *last*, chance to consider your options. It is now 2:00AM on Monday in Moscow, 1:00AM in Kiev. I am going to give you 48 hours to rethink your country's position and begin your withdrawal from Ukraine. As you must have learned by now, we are capable of watching every move you make, be it in the light of day or in the middle of the night.

"The majority of your Army materiel has been destroyed. Leave it where it lies. What is left must retreat to Russia. As for your aircraft, what wasn't destroyed is

144

stuck on the ground as the airfield where they sit cannot be used until the runway is repaired. You may negotiate the ultimate return of the surviving aircraft with President Poroshenko or whoever may succeed him.

"Finally, as regards your brave young men who take their orders from you and your subordinates. They are to leave Ukraine by whatever means possible. We will be watching. And we will be talking to our sources on the ground in Ukraine."

"Your spies you mean," interrupted Putin.

"Whatever," said Jefferson. "In the meantime, should you attempt to replace your military weaponry or aircraft, we will take this as a sign of non-compliance. And should you introduce additional troops into Ukraine, they will surely die, as will those who survived our first attack. To lose so many young lives would be a tragedy for their mothers, their families, and for the Russian Federation.

"If, in 48 hours, our reconnaissance does not reflect a move to withdraw all military assets from Ukraine, I will order our forces to finish the job we started today. Have I made myself clear?" asked Jefferson.

"Your intentions are as clear as always," said Putin.

"Good," closed Jefferson. "I hope you heed them."

When Jefferson got off the phone with President Putin, he called General Milley on the Pentagon's line.

"Mark," he began, "John Jefferson here. I just got off the phone with Putin. I told him he had 48 hours for his troops and mechanized weaponry to exhibit their intentions of returning to Russia. I also informed him that they would be under constant surveillance, both from the air and on the ground. That last part rattled him a bit."

"I'll bet it did," remarked General Milley.

"Anyway," resumed Jefferson, "I'm going to hold firmly to that 48-hour timeline. I spoke to him at 2:00AM Moscow time, 1:00AM Kiev time. I've looped Kessel Run in on the raw intel coming out of the 24th IS without it having to go through ACC headquarters. Make sure that you're in that same loop. If the analysts at Ramstein report no substantive movement of the Russians toward home after having observed them through late Tuesday evening, I want you to have our forces en route, prepared to enter Ukrainian airspace at precisely 1:00AM Wednesday morning. I have no intention of losing the life of a single American airman or Marine. Nor do I want to be reduced to writing a letter of condolences to a single grieving family."

"Understood, Sir," said Milley. "Our aircraft will be deployed in time to enter Ukrainian airspace at 0100 hours."

Chapter Nineteen

Monday and Tuesday saw a flurry of activity in
Washington, Moscow, and around the world. In New York,
the United Nations' Security Council received numerous
formal letters of protest against the Russians for their
invasion of Ukraine with the intention of ultimately re-
annexing what they considered to be nothing more than a
rogue republic. They also received a significant number of
protests against the Americans' attack on the Russian
military from countries still within the sphere of influence of
the Eastern Bloc. Finally, countries in the West were issuing
statements and their press writing editorials condemning
Russia for its wanton attacks on the Ukrainians who were
still, nearly three decades later, trying to claw their way to
first world status after being a subservient member of the
Soviet bloc for the seven decades from 1919 until 1991.
Especially pointed protests were emanating from the nations
of both the European Union and NATO who viewed Ukraine
as a novice in waiting to each of their alliances.

Another troublesome reaction was that of Recep
Erdoğan, President of Turkey. No sooner had Vladimir
Putin learned that *Raptors* flying from Incirlik Air Base in
Turkey had been part of the air assault on the Russian troops
in Ukraine than he picked up the phone and called Erdoğan.
He had made it clear to him in no uncertain terms that no
more American aircraft were to be allowed to take off from

Incirlik for the duration of the hostilities. In response, Erdoğan had the electricity shut down to all the buildings occupied, either as offices or housing, by Americans. He placed well-armed Turkish Army troops around the perimeter of the base where American aircraft were hangared or parked on the tarmac with orders to shoot if those aircraft were approached. Finally, orders were issued to all staff in the control tower not to let any American aircraft take off *or* land. This created an immediate problem for American military aircraft being redeployed throughout the Middle East, but with some ingenuity and the emergency use of air-to-air refueling, all aircraft got on the ground safely.

The Russian invasion became the focal point of the presidential campaigns of the three viable candidates among the 44 whose names appeared on the ballot for the highest elected post in Ukraine. Volodymyr Zelensky, the actor and comedian who had once played the Ukrainian President in a television sitcom, attacked Petro Poroshenko mercilessly for letting the Russians get away with the incursion onto sovereign Ukrainian soil at the same time as Ukraine was making serious overtures to join both the EU and NATO. In criticism from yet another source, Yulia Tymoshenko pulled no punches in her critique of Poroshenko's failure to eliminate the government corruption which was one of his two main campaign issues in his first election.

President Jefferson found himself in multiple

meetings on both Monday and Tuesday with Secretary of State Wainwright as well as delegations of both Republicans and Democrats from Capitol Hill. While Wainwright stood steadfast with the President in his unwavering condemnation of Vladimir Putin and the Russian Federation, the Republicans and Democrats, as could have been expected, found themselves on opposite sides of the geopolitical fence.

This was all becoming somewhat tedious for President Jefferson, and by Noon on Tuesday, 7:00PM in Kiev, he'd had enough. He instructed his Appointments Secretary to clear his calendar for the remainder of the day. He invited the Joint Chiefs to join him for a late lunch that afternoon in the Situation Room where they could monitor last-minute developments in the six hours leading up to zero hour.

General Milley got on to Air Force Brigadier General Mark August, Commander of Ramstein Air Base, and told him that he wanted live feeds routed to the Situation Room, on split screen when appropriate, of all the raw intel coming into the 24th Intelligence Squadron from all the ISR platforms monitoring both ground and air activity in Ukraine. He, as did the President, wanted to see for himself the activity or lack thereof of Russian military assets in Ukraine in the final hours before condemning thousands of Russian airmen, soldiers, and possibly sailors to their deaths.

Only those who have served in combat, as had Milley,

knew the horror of war. They would do whatever possible to avoid it. Milley had served in the 82nd Airborne Division and the 5th Special Forces Group during Operation *Iraqi Freedom* and Operation *Enduring Freedom* in Afghanistan. If the evidence coming out of the 24th IS showed that the Russians were withdrawing from Ukraine, Milley would be the first among the Joint Chiefs to counsel the President against a second attack.

* * *

Seven time zones to the East, both the Russian and American Air Forces were contending with unanticipated dilemmas. The Russians needed a new base of operations for Russian aircraft within Ukraine while the Americans' F-22 *Raptors* now trapped on the ground at Incirlik would no longer be able to help fly escort for the two B-1B *Lancers* flying in from Qatar. A good number of the airports in Ukraine are jointly operated by the Ukrainian Air Force and the government authorities for the accommodation of civilian airlines. The Russians saw no reason to provoke a battle on both the ground and in the air over a landing field for their aircraft in Ukraine. Consequently, they chose a civilian airport which was convenient for aircraft flying in from Russia.

Although it was nearly 200 miles Northeast of their original aviation operations center and over 200 miles from their command and control center in central Ukraine, the

Russian Air Force chose Kharkiv International Airport as their new base of operations. It was closer to the Russian border and home to two runways, one 8,202 feet of concrete and the other 4,921 feet of asphalt. And it was operated by civilian authorities. A good portion of the Russian Army troops and equipment which had originally rolled into Kharkiv to subdue it would be moved to the airport over the next 48 hours and the majority of the mobile SAM missile launchers which had been deployed on the outskirts of Kharkiv would be relocated to the perimeter of the airport.

With their entire fleet of aircraft which were originally committed to the war in Ukraine having been destroyed or stranded except for those airborne at the time of the attack, the Russians had to fly in an entirely new fleet of MiG-31s and Su-57s. Those MiG-31s which had been enforcing the no-fly zone were able to either make it back to Russian airspace and land at a military airfield or land at the Novofedorivka Naval Air Station in Crimea. They would eventually rejoin the Russian occupying fleet.

As for the American *Raptors*, their role in escorting the *Lancers* would have to be picked up by either more of the *Fighting Falcons* from Aviano or by some of the *Super Hornets* off the deck of the *Truman*. General Goldfein, the Air Force Chief of Staff, in consultation with Admiral Richardson, the CNO, had deemed it a good idea that additional F-16s be added to the escort tasking as, although both aircraft were designed to sustain a 9.0 g-load making them equally maneuverable in aerial combat, the F-18 had a top speed of only 1,190 mph at altitude while the F-16 could reach 1,320.

This meant that more of the load of carrying and dropping the BLU-129/Bs would be assigned to the *Super Hornets*. Once again, the SNIPER app from Kessel Run would have to be called upon to change the distribution of VLCDWs en route to the theater of operations while the *Globemaster IIIs* were in the air. More of the warheads would need to be delivered to Naval Air Station Sigonella to be ferried to the deck of the *Truman* by their *Greyhounds* while fewer would need to be deployed to Aviano. SNIPER would spit out the exact numbers and they would be forwarded to the C-17s and the Aviation Ordnance Loaders.

While all of this activity was going on, the President and the Joint Chiefs were keeping up with it in real time on flat panel screens in the Situation Room. The clock was ticking down to 6:00PM, 1:00AM Wednesday morning in Ukraine. The crucial moment for the "Go – No Go" call was fast approaching. Once the *Lancers*, *Fighting Falcons*, and *Super Hornets* entered Ukrainian airspace, the die would be cast and the battle joined. By 4:00PM the *Lancers* from Qatar would be airborne and the *Fighting Falcons* would leave Aviano shortly after 5:00. The *Super Hornets* would be the last to take off so as to not prematurely tip America's hand as they overflew the warships of Russia's Black Sea Fleet. The President and Joint Chiefs watched, and waited.

Chapter Twenty

By 5:47PM, Chairman Milley had seen enough. After a momentary consultation with the assembled members of the Joint Chiefs, he turned to President Jefferson and said, "It's time, Sir. President Putin is remaining true to his word. The only signs of the withdrawal of troops or weaponry from any city have taken place in Kharkiv where a portion of those assets have been redeployed to Kharkiv International Airport to safeguard the MiG-31 and Su-57 fighters which have been flown in from Russia to replace those destroyed or grounded after our first strike."

"Let's do it then," replied Jefferson. "Get the word out that I want our F-16s, F-18s, and B-1Bs to penetrate Ukrainian airspace at the stroke of 1:00AM Kiev time. All the aircraft should have been loaded with the prescribed ordnance and now be approaching Ukraine. Each pilot will already have received his air target charts showing him his designated targets. The plan of battle is to be executed just as we discussed."

"Roger that, Sir," said Milley.

He got on one of the numerous secure lines in the Situation Room, this one to the Air Operations Centers around the world, and issued the order.

"The aircraft currently headed for Ukraine are to penetrate Ukrainian airspace at 0100 local time. Their targets remain as assigned at their pre-flight briefings."

General Milley received confirmation of his orders from the AOCs at Aviano, Al Udeid, and aboard the *Truman*.

"It's done, Sir," said the Chairman, hanging up the phone and turning to the President. "We'll be able to monitor the progress of the raids in real time on these screens. If, at any time, you want to focus on one objective, just give the word and I'll make it so."

"God bless," said Jefferson. "And God bless each and every one of our men in harm's way. Now let's kick some Russian ass!"

The first aircraft to enter Ukrainian airspace were the two B-1B *Lancers* with their escorts of F-16 *Fighting Falcons* from Aviano's 510th Buzzards and 555th Triple Nickels. Their first objective was Kharkiv International Airport. All the aircraft had flipped on the electronic countermeasures in their avionics systems and were transmitting full blast to confuse the relatively primitive targeting systems of the Russian mobile SAM launchers.

As with their first attack on the airfield in central Ukraine, the Aviation Ordnance Loaders at Al Udeid had arranged the bombs so that the first ones to be released by the two *Lancers* were the 12 GBU-31 Joint Direct Attack Munition GPS-guided JDAMs from each of their bomb bays. The majority of them would be dropped on the clusters of fighter jets outside a number of the commandeered hangars while the remainder would be dropped at critical points on the principle 8,202-foot concrete runway.

The asphalt runway was just marginally long enough to handle the MiG-31, but, unlike the concrete one which had just been resurfaced, its structural integrity had been compromised over the years and it was questionable whether it could withstand either the takeoff or landing of a high-performance military jet. As for handling the Su-57, it was less than half the weight of the MiG-31 but, as the latest fifth-generation stealth multirole fighter in the Russian arsenal, the military authorities were not inclined to risk one of their prized possessions on a dilapidated asphalt runway. Thus, disabling the principle runway would serve the Americans' purpose.

Because the Russians had been reduced to utilizing a civilian airfield from which to operate the airborne element of their assault upon Ukraine, the commercial-grade radar equipment in the control tower had not given them adequate warning of the approach of the *Lancers* and their *Fighting Falcons* escort to scramble either their MiG-31s or Su-57s before the first bombs landed. As planned, a good number of the fighter aircraft on the ground were either destroyed or disabled and the main runway had been damaged to such an extent that it could not safely be used to get the surviving fighters airborne. In fact, the American bombers and fighters were flying so fast that the whine of their blazing jet engines was not heard on the ground until after the JDAMs had detonated.

Thus, for the time being, any attack on the American aircraft in Ukrainian airspace would be left to the MiG-31s attempting to enforce the no-fly zone. The call went out from the command and control center in central Ukraine to all the MiGs aloft to converge upon the Kharkiv airport. Updates on the American aircraft locations and direction of flight would be provided as they became available.

After the bombing of the airport, one detachment of F-16s headed for downtown Kharkiv while the others remained with the B-1Bs and circled back for a second run on the airfield. This time their targets were not the parked aircraft or the runway but the mobile SAM launchers, tanks & artillery, and troops of the Russian Army which had been redeployed from the city to the airport. They came in low and were primed for the kill.

On this run, the *Lancers* were each dropping their 42 BLU-129/Bs on the machines and men which they aimed to destroy and kill respectively. The F-16s let the B-1Bs unload their ordnance first on low-speed passes. Once they had done so, they rotated their wings so that they were flush with their fuselages, accelerated to maximum speed, and climbed to their service ceiling of 60,000 feet to await their escort out of Ukrainian airspace.

It wasn't that the MiGs couldn't reach them there, for they had service ceilings of 82,000 feet, but rather that as they arrived on station they would be focused upon the aircraft actively making bombing runs on Russian troops and equipment. As each of the *Fighting Falcons* made its bombing run in the vicinity of the airport, it dropped its BLU-129/Bs on the relocated Russian tanks and equipment, as well as on the men manning them. This time around, human lives were part of the target package.

After the F-16s made their bombing run, they turned and made one more low-level run, this time unloading their *Vulcan* 6-barrel 20mm rotary cannons on the soldiers fleeing the fire and destruction of their equipment. It was like shooting so many fish in a barrel. Those men who had not been immolated in their tanks or killed in the explosions of their artillery batteries were cut down as they fled.

The ground around the perimeter of the airport was slowly becoming saturated with human blood and scattered with dismembered limbs. It was growing to be as gruesome as the scenes of some of the battles during the Siege of Leningrad during World War II. Blessedly, the F-16s finally ran out of cannon rounds and they departed the scene, climbing nearly vertically to rejoin their charges, the two B-

1Bs, which had descended to 50,000 feet, the *Fighting Falcon's* service ceiling.

As they turned South to put the *Lancers* on their path to Qatar, the formation found itself with a flight of four MiG-31s on its six. The pilots in the F-16s and B-1Bs were among the best the Air Force had to offer. But their aircraft were no match for the MiG-31s.

The American aircraft formation included two *Lancers* flying side by side accompanied by four *Fighting Falcons*, two to their left and two to their right. When the pilots detected the MiGs, each of the B-1Bs which had been flying at their max speed of Mach 1.25 with their four GE F101 turbofan jets went to afterburners which provided 30,780 foot-pounds of thrust each. They remained flying straight ahead on the heading which would take them out of Ukrainian airspace in the shortest amount of time possible.

To their left and right, the inner two F-16s went to afterburners and dove for the floor while the two outer ones ignited their afterburners and went vertical. The tactic was pure textbook, but the *Fighting Falcons* were simply over-matched by the MiGs. Both of the aircraft were designed and built to withstand 9g-loads in their turns, climbs, and dives. But the F-16s had single GE F110-GE-129 turbofan jet engines which yielded a maximum speed of 1,320 miles per hour and generated 28,600 foot-pounds of thrust each when pushed to afterburner. The MiGs, by contrast, had two

Soloviev D-30-F6 turbofan jet engines which provided them with a top speed of 1,860 miles per hour and generated 34,172 foot-pounds of thrust each on afterburner.

Moreover, the MiGs had been hung with 4 R-60 short-range lightweight infrared-homing air-to-air missiles. They were supplemented by 4 R-33 air-to-air missiles which had been designed to attack large high-speed targets such as the SR-71 *Blackbird*, the B-52 *Stratofortress*, and, most importantly, the B-1B *Lancer* bomber.

Two of the MiGs dove to pursue the two F-16s on the deck while the other two climbed to pull in behind the rocketing F-16s. With speeds that exceeded those of the *Fighting Falcons* by in excess of 500 miles per hour, all four of the MiGs were in firing position within less than a minute. The two diving MiGs were traveling at speeds in excess of 2,000 miles per hour. They each fired one of their R-60s which themselves were propelled by their solid-fuel rocket engines to a speed of Mach 2.7.

Fortunately, the warning tones in the cockpits of the two low-level F-16s had sounded as soon as the MiGs' missiles' targeting computers had locked on to the heat signatures of their engines running on afterburner. It only took a fraction of a second for the pilots to conclude that their only means of escape was to eject. They both pulled their ejection levers and were rocketed free of their aircraft's fuselages only seconds before they were destroyed by the incoming R-60s' 6.6-pound high explosive warheads.

Two parachutes were soon drifting down in the nearly moonless night sky into the farm fields of Southern Ukraine. When the pilots hit the ground, they were quickly surrounded by groups of Ukrainian farmers who had been awakened by the noise of the aerial combat and had left their houses to see what all the commotion was about. Instantly recognizing that the pilots were Americans, the Ukrainians got them into one of their barns where they would be provided with cover, food, and drink for the duration of the war.

The two MiGs chasing the climbing F-16s closed rapidly on their quarry. They targeted them with their R-60s as quickly as possible as their air-to-air missiles' service ceiling was 66,000 feet. But before the targeting computers could lock on to the F-16s' heat signatures and their tones could blare in the MiGs' cockpits, both of the F-16s, running rich on afterburners, flamed out. As they had exceeded their service ceilings, the oxygen in the surrounding atmosphere had grown too thin. Traveling nearly vertically, the F-16s both stalled and each fell into a dead spin.

Fortunately for the two pilots, the aircraft's control surfaces still functioned. One of the pilots was able to stabilize his plane's attitude and he put it into a steep glide as he struggled with the controls until the F-16 dropped below 50,000 feet. Then he continually tried to restart his engine until the oxygen-to-fuel ratio reached the point where he could regain the ability to resume the combustion of the mixture. His first instinct was to come to the aid of his fellow F-16 pilot. But the MiG on his tail had never broken off the chase. He had resumed the attack and was soon once again on the six of the F-16. His aircraft's targeting computer's tone sounded and he prepared to fire his R-60. Fortunately for the American pilot, his radar told him he was being "painted" and he safely ejected before the MiG fired its missile. Seconds later he heard the roar as his F-16 exploded below him. He floated safely to the soil of the rich farmland where he was given shelter in the same manner as the two previous pilots.

Unfortunately, the fourth pilot was never able to regain attitude control of his plane and it continued to spin rapidly. Without the proper airflow through the turbines, restarting the engine was out of the question. In a last-ditch effort to save himself, he pulled the ejection lever. The canopy blew off the fuselage and his ejection seat rocketed skyward. But just as he cleared the cockpit, the single vertical stabilizer of his aircraft's tail assembly slammed into his ejection seat. The concussion of the impact killed the pilot instantly before his seat's parachute ever had a chance to open.

The MiGs' pursuit of the four F-16s had provided the *Lancers* with time to build up a large enough gap between themselves and the MiGs that they reached international airspace before the pursuing Russian aircraft could catch up to them. But, just as a precaution, the CAG on board the *Truman* who had been monitoring the radio traffic among the pilots had launched four of his F-18 *Super Hornets*. They had rendezvoused with the two B-1Bs just off the Southern coast of Ukraine and would fly escort until all five aircraft reached Al Udeid.

In a matter of no more than ten minutes, the United States Air Force had lost $75.2 million worth of hardware. But that could all be replaced. This was the first American life to be lost in the United States' pursuit of continued independence for Ukraine. A life that could *never* be replaced.

Chapter Twenty-one

Once the flight of four F-16s had broken off from the formation escorting the B-1Bs to the airport, it had taken them only moments to arrive over the city center of Kharkiv itself just Northwest of the airfield. The situation was exactly as the imagery analysts had observed on the last pass of the KH-13 satellite and their air target charts reflected. Now *all* of the Russian equipment and men not redeployed to the airport had been positioned in the immediate vicinity of four of Kharkiv's most significant religious landmarks.

The first was the St. Annunciation Orthodox Cathedral, one of the tallest Orthodox churches in the world. Its construction had been completed in 1888. The second landmark was St. Mary's Roman Catholic Cathedral which was completed in 1892. The third was the Kharkiv Choral Synagogue whose renovation had just been completed in 2016. And the fourth was the Kharkiv Cathedral Mosque. To inflict damage on any of these edifices would elicit an outcry not only from Ukrainians but from Russians as well.

The targeting with the BLU-129/Bs "dumb" bombs would have to be of the highest precision. In order for the pilots of the F-16s to select and hit their targets with the greatest accuracy to prevent damaging the religious sites, they would have to fly low and slow. Since all the mobile SAM missile launchers which Russia had allocated to

Kharkiv had been redeployed, and subsequently destroyed, at the airport, they were of no concern. And the artillery batteries could simply not react quickly enough to be of any significant threat.

The F-16 had a stall speed of roughly 200 miles per hour. That meant that as long as they maintained level flight at above that speed, they would stay aloft. For reference, 200 miles per hour is about the speed at which a NASCAR race car travels on the high-banked superspeedways such as Daytona and Talladega.

The flight of four F-16s descended above their four target areas. They leveled out and slowed as much as they prudently could without the risk of losing their aircraft. Each would make three runs, dropping two of its VLCDWs on each run. Then, they would make one last run expending all the rounds in their 20mm 6-barrel rotary cannons. After those fourth passes, the four F-16s would climb to their service ceiling of 50,000 feet and head due West to be refueled by a KC-135 *Stratotanker* from the 100th ARW once they departed Ukrainian airspace and make for home at Aviano.

All four pilots were right on the money, inflicting the maximum possible damage on the Russian guns and tanks on each of their first three passes. Their final pass was reserved for taking out as many of the enemy combatants as possible before their ammunition was exhausted. They then climbed to what they deemed to be a safe altitude and turned to the West.

Unfortunately, a flight of four MiG-31s which had been at the far Western perimeter of the Ukrainian no-fly zone was headed due East at 60,000 feet in response to the call for all available fighter aircraft to converge upon the Kharkiv airport. They picked up the F-16s on their radar and went into attack mode. In the pitch black night sky, the F-16s never saw them coming.

The MiG pilots waited until the F-16s had passed beneath them and then went into tight 9g turns to pull up behind them. Each MiG picked out a *Fighting Falcon.* They locked their firing computers on the heat signatures of each F-16's GE-F110 turbofan jet engine. Only then did the F-16 pilots know that they were being painted. But, before they could react, the Russian flight leader gave the command and each MiG unleashed an R-60 air-to-air missile which accelerated to Mach 2.7 and hit its mark.

Three of the four F-16s were destroyed instantly. Only the fourth was still recognizable as an aircraft, but it was rotating wildly due to the loss of its tail assembly and, consequently, its control surfaces. The MiG which had taken the first shot fired a second R-60 and the remaining F-16 disintegrated. The four MiGs had to climb to avoid being struck by the flying debris from the four destroyed aircraft.

Due to the lack of enemy aircraft in the vicinity, the four Air Force *Fighting Falcons* from Aviano which had been assigned to strike the Russian Army encampments in Kiev were able to conduct their raid successfully with a minimum of resistance from the Russian artillery batteries. All the principal targets were destroyed and a significant number of Russian Army troops eliminated. Just as with the flight which had struck Kharkiv, they headed West to refuel and return to Italy.

As always, the CAG aboard the *Truman* had been monitoring the radio chatter among the Air Force pilots. Even before he had sent the flight of four F-18 *Super Hornets* to escort the two *Lancers* back to Qatar, he had made an executive decision which was well above his pay grade and which could easily prevent him ever receiving another promotion if not getting him drummed out of the Navy. But his heart and soul had always been with his pilots, not the political admirals.

At the last minute, before his two flights of four *Super Hornets* each were to take off from the deck of the *Truman* for Kropyvnytskyi and Odessa, he had reached a conclusion. The aircraft which the Russians had at their disposal were simply technologically superior to anything which the Americans were bringing to the fight. The planes were all equally maneuverable, and their armament was well-matched. However, the Russians had more raw power and were merciless in their pursuit of enemy blood.

But there was one element which, to date, had not been a factor in the air-to-air combat; *stealth*. In the first raid on Kryvyi Rih International Airport on the morning of Sunday, May 3rd, any available Russian Su-57 fifth-generation stealth fighters had been stranded on the ground when the runway was damaged and became unusable for takeoff. By the same token, all the American fifth-generation stealth F-22 *Raptors* on the runways at Incirlik had been grounded by order of Turkish President Erdoğan at the request of Russian President Putin.

However. the CAG had four four-aircraft flights of America's newest weapon in its arsenal, the F-35C *Lightning II* stealth multirole fighter which had only been certified by the Navy as "ready for combat" from the deck of an aircraft carrier seven days earlier. He'd sent his two flights of *Super Hornets* below deck on the carrier's elevators and told the Aviation Ordnance Loaders he wanted eight *Lightning IIs* hung with BLU-129/Bs and ready for takeoff ASAP. On an aircraft carrier, an order from the CAG was like the voice of God, and they had made it so.

One by one, the *Lightning IIs* rose to the deck on the aft elevator. As the first rolled into position for takeoff, the other seven lined up behind. Then, one by one, the F-35Cs roared off the deck headed North for Kropyvnytskyi and Odessa. Flying at 1,200 miles per hour in stealth mode at their service ceiling of 50,000 feet, they flew over and past the cordon of Black Sea Fleet ships off the Southern coast of Ukraine totally unnoticed.

When the two flights arrived above Odessa, the first went into orbit mode to give the second time to reach Kropyvnytskyi. They wanted to strike both the Russian Command and Control Center and Odessa at the same time. To have struck Odessa first would have given the entire Russian military contingent in Ukraine a heads up and the opportunity to adjust their tactics accordingly.

Fifteen minutes later, the second flight was in position. Each of the *Lightning IIs* had been hung with eight BLU-129/Bs, six on their external hardpoints and two in their internal bays. They would each make four runs dropping two VLCDWs on each run. On their fifth and final run, they would empty their 4-barrel 20mm *Equalizer* rotary cannons on the fleeing troops.

But while the F-35s had been making their way North and getting into position, the Russian's MiGs had not been standing idly by. Two of their four target cities had been hit. They knew an attack on the other two was imminent. Consequently, they had passed the order that half of the airborne MiGs converge on Kropyvnytskyi while the other half headed for Odessa. This was to be the *battle royale* of the conflict. Not only was the CAG's ass and career on the line, but so was the legitimacy of the much-vaunted claim of America's military might as the world's only superpower.

Kessel Run

Chapter Twenty-two

The stealthiness of all three variants of the F-35 *Lightning II* is a function of both the unconventional angles of the aircraft's exterior surfaces coupled with the radar-absorbent fiber-mat and other stealthy materials applied to the external surfaces of the aircraft. The three variants, the F-35A, B, and C are all designed to be used in different environments.

The F-35A is the most conventional variant in the F-35 family. Designed to replace the Air Force's F-16 *Fighting Falcon*, it is the smallest and lightest version and is the only variant equipped with the GAU-22/A *Vulcan* 4-barrel 25mm internal rotary cannon designed to provide increased effectiveness against ground targets. It is comparable in both maneuverability and instantaneous high-g performance to the *Fighting Falcon* and can outperform it in stealth, payload, range on internal fuel, avionics, operational effectiveness, supportability, and survivability.

The F-35B is the short takeoff and vertical landing variant of the aircraft. While comparable in size to the A variant, the B carries roughly one-third less fuel as it sacrifices fuel tank volume to the vertical flight system. Unlike other variants, the F-35B has no landing hook. The F-35B's jet thrust is directed downwards during vertical flight. The variant's three-bearing swivel nozzle that directs the full thrust of the engine is moved by a "fueldraulic" actuator using pressurized fuel as the working fluid.

The F-35C is the carrier variant. It sports larger wings, larger wing and tail control surfaces for enhanced low-speed control, and foldable wingtip sections for storage either on deck or below decks on an aircraft carrier. It also features beefed-up landing gear to allow it to withstand the increased stresses of aircraft carrier arrested landings, twin-wheel nose gear, and a stronger tailhook to capture the carrier's arrestor cables.

For Sunday's impromptu mission off the deck of the *Truman*, the CAG had launched eight F-35Cs. They would be going up against the Russian MiGs above Kropyvnytskyi and Odessa. The MiGs out-manned the *Lightning IIs* by one crew member, carrying a weapons systems officer (WSO) in the rear seat, out-powered it by one jet engine, outraced it by over 600 miles per hour at maximum speed, and outdistanced it by150 miles in combat radius. But the F-35C had one thing going for it. It had stealth.

There was one variable which inevitably compromised the characteristics of any stealth fighter. That was the ordnance hung on its external hardpoints. Be they missiles or bombs, the housings were almost always constructed of steel, one of the strongest reflectors of radar waves. While the fuselage and wings were covered with radar-absorbing and/or radar-refracting materials, the missiles and bombs were not.

But this was not just any mission. Because the decision had been made at the highest levels to do everything possible to prevent damage to infrastructure or loss of life in the four cities where the Russians had taken up positions, BLU-129/B Very Low Collateral Damage Weapons had been ordered used rather than standard ordnance. The principal reason the VLCDWs did so little damage other than to the target it struck was that its housing was made of composite carbon fiber which vaporizes when the warhead is detonated, thereby dispersing no shrapnel. And carbon fiber, unlike steel, is known to be a poor reflector of radar waves. In fact, some theorize that it is may even be a radar-absorbing material.

It was still hours before sunrise on the nearly moonless night when the F-35Cs arrived on station at their respective targets. They radioed into the Combat Information Center (CIC) aboard the *Truman* that they were preparing to commence their bombing runs. That information had been forwarded to the Air Force E-4 *Nightwatch* aircraft which had been orbiting at 45,000 feet above the theater of operations since the day after the Russian troops had rolled into Ukraine.

The F-35Cs descended from their service ceiling of 50,000 feet above both Kropyvnytskyi and Odessa and picked up their targets on radar. The four to the Northeast headed toward the Russian command and control center while those to the South took aim at downtown Odessa. There were eight MiGs in the air, four each circling both Kropyvnytskyi and Odessa, but so far the F-35Cs had eluded detection.

The *Lightning IIs*, which had been flying in formation, lined up nose to tail. As the train of aircraft approached the target area, each aircraft took up a heading which would take it to its first target. Because the F-35C was designed specifically for use on aircraft carriers, and because it would be landing in a variety of wind and sea conditions, it had been designed with a very low stall speed.

The F-35Cs all slowed simultaneously to their minimum flight speed, that which they used when landing upon a carrier's deck, and began their target runs. The first sign the MiGs had of their presence is when the first BLU-129/Bs detonated as they struck their first targets. Their flight paths became evident when the second bomb exploded.

The MiG pilots instantly extrapolated from those two points the flight paths of each of the F-35Cs. But the American flight leaders in both Kropyvnytskyi and Odessa had briefed their pilots that upon dropping their second bombs they were to alternate breaking left and right and circle around using a maximum g-force turn before climbing to 2500 feet and lining up for their second run. The MiGs raced to where they believed the F-35Cs' heading would take them, but they were nowhere to be found. The electronic countermeasure/warfare system on the *Lightning II* was the most sophisticated ever developed. Designed by BAE, the AN/ASQ-239 suite was the world's most advanced electronic warfare system.

The AN/ASQ-239 suite provides the F-35 with protection using both offensive and defensive electronic warfare options for the pilot and aircraft. It furnishes fully integrated radar warning, targeting support, and self-protection to detect and defeat both surface and airborne threats. Providing the pilot with maximum situational awareness, it helps to identify, monitor, analyze, and respond to potential threats.

The system's advanced avionics and sensors provide a real-time, 360-degree view of the battlespace and maximizes detection ranges, thereby providing the pilot with options to evade, engage, counter, or jam threats. The AN/ASQ-239 is always active and supplies the F-35 with all-aspect broadband protection using radio-frequency and infrared countermeasures, maximizing the pilot's capability of responding rapidly.

The radar systems on the Russian mobile SAM launchers searched the skies for targets but found none. However, the missile officers had also estimated where they thought the *Lightning IIs* would be and commanded the men staffing the batteries to commence firing nonetheless. The sky was soon filled with surface-to-air missiles whose heat-seeking targeting systems were trying in vain to locate targets. Unfortunately for the MiG pilots, their aircraft put out glaringly hot heat signatures from their twin jet engines. The outcome was inevitable.

Above Odessa, two of the SAMs found suitable targets, slamming into two of the MiG-31s and sending them crashing into the sides of high-rise government office buildings in the city center before their pilots and WSOs ever had the chance to eject. In Kropyvnytskyi, the SAMs found only one target. The lone MiG crashed in a farm field, but the pilot and WSO were fortunate enough to survive, ejecting and floating to Earth in the pre-dawn Ukrainian sky. Their fate at the hands of the Ukrainians would lead them to wonder if their survival had indeed constituted good fortune.

The four-aircraft flights of F-35Cs made their second and third bombing runs successfully and without incident. But the Russians were becoming familiar with their aerial tactics and both the MiG pilots and SAM launcher crews were just skilled enough to anticipate the *Lightning IIs'* paths of flight and adjust their responses accordingly. This time the MiGs were maintaining their orbits at 5,000 feet awaiting the F-35Cs' next run.

Chapter Twenty-three

Neither the MiG pilots nor the SAM launch crews could outguess where the *Lightning IIs* would strike next, but they *could* respond more appropriately once the eight VLCDWs had detonated on their targets in both Kropyvnytskyi and Odessa. The MiGs stayed well aloft while the launchers unleashed deadly volleys of heat-seeking missiles as soon as, and in the direction of, the light from the explosions appeared. Not only did the SAMs chase the F-35Cs, but they also served the same function as tracer bullets in providing a trail for the MiGs to follow.

The MiGs pursued the yellowish-orange rocket exhaust from the SAMs in much the same way as a state trooper would pursue the taillights of a speeding vehicle racing down the highway in front of them. The MiGs' R-60 air-to-air missiles were designed to seek out a heat signature from an aircraft's jet engine, not a small SAM's solid fuel rocket. And there was nothing a fleeing F-35C's pilot could do to diminish his engine's heat signature.

The F-35Cs' AN/ASQ-239's electronic countermeasures could do their best to distract the MiGs' targeting computers, but the SAMs just kept on coming. And behind them came the MiGs. As the SAMs' rockets flamed out before striking their targets, the MiG WSOs fired their R-60s. In Kropyvnytskyi, two of the three remaining

MiGs' missiles missed their mark, but both R-60s from the third struck the trailing F-35C, tearing it into several parts. When his warning system ceased sounding after the rockets flamed out, the pilot had thought he was in the clear and momentarily relaxed. That brief lapse in attentiveness ended up costing him his life. Had he been aware of the closing R-60s, he could have ejected in a timely manner, but the interval between awareness and action was just a tad too short.

In Odessa, the Russians employed the same tactic, but there they were working with one less MiG. As a result, there were only two MiGs to follow four sets of "taillights". Unfortunately, there had not been enough lead time between the events in Kropyvnytskyi and the MiGs' attack in Odessa to allow for the American pilots to radio their comrades about the scheme being employed by the Russians. As a result, the outcome was the same.

After dropping the last of their eight bombs, each of the four F-35Cs had broken left and right alternately. Thus, the trailing SAM rockets had done the same. One MiG broke left while the other broke right. The SAMs which had followed the F-35Cs to the left flamed out and the trailing MiG fired all of his remaining R-60s into what one could call the "center mass" of the cluster. Passing through the cloud of now-coasting SAMs, one of the R-60s found its mark.

The *Lightning II* was destroyed, but the pilot had had adequate warning of the approaching missile to safely eject. He ended up landing on the roof of one of Odessa's numerous Eastern Orthodox churches. When the priest inside heard the clatter on the rooftop, he arose from bed, donned his robe and slippers, and went to see what all the ruckus was about.

From the edge of the second-floor balcony he could see the American airman. He motioned with his hands for the pilot to lower himself down the steep roof and onto the balcony. The ejection seat had slid down the roof into the street below, but the parachute had caught on the church's steeple. Thus, the pilot had reached for the combat knife in its ankle sheath and was cutting the paracord lines which were holding the parachute in place. If he didn't get it off the roof, it would be like sending a message to the MiGs aloft that "X" marks the spot. He finally cut the last of the lines, pulled the parachute down the roof, and then descended to the safety of the balcony where he joined the priest and ducked inside before his location could be pinpointed. The two then climbed down the stairs to the ground floor, exited the church into the street, and together dragged the ejection seat indoors before its presence could be detected. The pilot then deactivated its locator signal.

In both Kropyvnytskyi and Odessa, the two American flight leaders prudently decided to forego their mop-up runs using their rotary cannons and commenced their stealthy race to the Ukrainian coast and the safety of the USS *Harry S. Truman*.

The destruction of the military hardware in both Kropyvnytskyi and Odessa had been complete. Only the random soldier remained. All told, the raids on the four cities had cost the Russians two pilots, two WSOs, and three MiG-31s while the loss to the Americans was six pilots, eight F-16s, and two F-35Cs. Such is the price of war.

With no more airborne American targets to engage, the remaining MiGs reassembled and then dispersed to resume their attempts at enforcing the Russian no-fly zone above Ukraine. Meanwhile, the surviving F-16s had all refueled and were making their way back to Aviano. Racing in front of the rising sun, the pilots would soon be in the officers' mess sipping coffee and mourning the loss of their five pilots killed after their raids on Kharkiv.

The F-35Cs' return to "base" was slightly more eventful. Although their stealth mode was holding, the Russian pilots aloft over both Kropyvnytskyi and Odessa had radioed the flagship of the Black Sea Fleet and alerted them that there were a number of American aircraft headed their way. While they were not inclined to waste any of their expensive rockets or missiles on shooting blind into the Ukrainian sky, the captains of the Russian ships ordered the sailors manning the artillery aboard the destroyers, cruisers, and frigates to periodically open fire with short bursts of ammunition in the hopes of striking the random American warplane in a crucial spot.

Nonetheless, all the aircraft made it through the Russian sieve-like dragnet and the six *Lightning IIs* were taking their turns making their arrestor-cable landings on the *Truman* far from shore in the heart of the Black Sea. One by one, the pilots made their way to the Ward Room where they gulped coffee, were served breakfast, and were methodically, one at a time, called into the Sensitive Compartmented Information Facility, or "SCIF", below decks to be debriefed by both the CAG and the carrier's intelligence officers.

SCIFs are, with the exception of the Situation Room in the White House, the most secure facilities within the military and intelligence communities where "raw" intelligence can be discussed. They exist at the Pentagon, the CIA, DIA, and NSA headquarters, at various sites around the country, and even in the Capitol. They also exist aboard aircraft carriers and at certain "black sites" around the world.

Entrance to a SCIF is gained by the user looking into a laser-guided retina scanning device which matches the pattern of blood vessels on the individual's retina to those in the computer database for that particular SCIF. They are located on military bases or civilian facilities on campuses protected by armed guards or have armed guards stationed at the entrance. Electronic information can be accessed from within the SCIF, but no electronic emissions can escape one. Consequently, electronic eavesdropping is impossible.

The value and sensitivity of raw intelligence cannot be overstated and its compromise can not only expose methods of intelligence collection but sources as well. Access to raw intelligence can reveal the sensitivity of a device used to photograph or eavesdrop on a facility where an enemy is conducting an illegal activity. But it can just as easily reveal the identity of an American spy or foreign national who has been recruited to betray his own country. Said another way, it can get people killed. It is also a place where ELINT (electronic intelligence), SIGINT (signals intelligence), and, most critically, HUMINT (human intelligence) can be collected, analyzed, and tactical or strategic plans devised.

Within hours, if not less, the information gleaned from the pilots who had overflown Ukraine and safely returned to base would be in the hands of both the Defense Intelligence Agency and the Joint Chiefs of Staff. Along with their intelligence analysts and officers, plans for the next steps in liberating Ukraine from Russian occupation would be "spitballed" by the Joint Chiefs, gamed out, contemplated, and formulated. The end result would then be presented to the President at a meeting of the National Security Council in the Situation Room of the White House before the sun ever came up in Washington that Wednesday morning.

Chapter Twenty-four

The sun wouldn't be rising until 6:34AM that morning, but President Jefferson gaveled the meeting in the Situation Room to order at 5:30. Before doing so he had left word for his Appointments Secretary to schedule a phone call with Russian President Putin for 9:00AM Washington time, 5:00PM Moscow time. He would place a call to President Poroshenko immediately before talking to Putin.

Present at the meeting in the Situation Room, in addition to the President, were the Vice President, all the members of the Joint Chiefs of Staff, Secretary of State Charles Wainwright, National Security Advisor Winnie Winstead, and the Directors of the DIA, CIA, and NSA. It took a few moments for all the players to end their side discussions and take their seats. When they had, President Jefferson began.

"Good morning, Ladies and Gentlemen," he started. "Before we begin the business of this meeting, I would like to have a moment of silence to recognize the bravery of our six pilots who lost their lives earlier today over Ukraine." The room fell into a hushed silence until the President resumed.

"Based upon the report I have received from Chairman Milley, we have achieved our objective.

Notwithstanding the loss of six American lives and ten aircraft, the Russian forces on the ground are in ruins. The tanks, artillery, and SAM launchers are, for the most part, either damaged or destroyed. A good number of the Army troops have been injured or killed. Most of the Russian aircraft on the ground are either damaged or disabled, and those which could fly are unable to do so for lack of a suitable runway for takeoff.

"As we had intended, there has been little to no damage to Ukrainian buildings or elements of their infrastructure due to our use of VLCDWs. And there has been minimal loss of Ukrainian lives. I am sure that the Russians are speculating as to what our next move will be. Determining *that* is the purpose of this meeting.

"Based upon what we decide here, I will be informing the Russians of their options when I speak with President Putin at 9:00AM. Immediately before that, I will be speaking with Ukrainian President Poroshenko to inform him of our plans. General Milley, would you please give us the latest update and the recommendation of you and your Joint Chiefs?"

"Thank you, Mister President," said Milley. "The Russian assets on the ground, be they Army or Air Force, are useless. The surviving soldiers and airmen have nothing with which to fight. And the Black Sea Fleet's impact upon the conflict has been non-existent.

"President Putin could continue to replenish the Russian forces in Ukraine indefinitely, but the mere expense would be staggering. Moreover, the cost in Russian lives would multiply. Finally, any appetite for war with Ukraine which may have existed among the Russian populace a week ago has, by now, rapidly waned. Russian mothers and fathers are increasingly reluctant to send their sons off to battle in a war they know they will inevitably lose.

"It is not possible to win a war with another country in the 21st century by means of air power alone. Although the Russian Air Force is a formidable adversary, as we have learned the hard way, the occupation and ultimate victory over a foe must be achieved by ground forces. Ukraine *could*, of course, surrender, but with the United States fighting their war for them, why would they?

"My recommendation, and that of the Joint Chiefs collectively, is that you tell Putin that as long as he continues to put Army equipment and troops on Ukrainian soil, we will destroy them. We can do this forever if necessary. We have studied their newest aerial combat tactics and our analysts are devising new maneuvers and measures to counteract them. In conclusion," wrapped up General Milley, "we recommend that you tell President Putin that we have won this round, and that we will win each successive round until he gives up his pursuit of re-annexing Ukrainian soil."

"Thank you, Chairman Milley," said Jefferson. "Secretary Wainwright, what have you been hearing through diplomatic channels?"

"Virtually everything I have been hearing since the Russian tanks rolled into Ukraine has been negative toward the Russians' intentions and positive with respect to our intervention," said Secretary of State Charles Wainwright. "All the members of the European Union which have taken sides have sided with us. Even our allies in the Middle East have been surprisingly vocal in their support of our actions. Only Russia's hard-line partners such as China and Iran have condemned us. And although he chose not to let us use Incirlik from which to launch attacks against Russian assets in Ukraine, Turkish President Recep Erdoğan has been rumored to have expressed his opinion that Russia's military adventurism in Ukraine is pure folly."

"Is there any reason why I should not simply inform President Putin that we have proven victorious and that any further incursions into Ukraine would meet with the same result?" Jefferson asked Wainwright.

"None that I can think of," replied the Secretary of State.

"What are your thoughts on the matter, Ms. Winstead?" asked Jefferson.

The National Security Advisor collected her thoughts and began.

"Well, Mister President," said Winstead, "you pay me to look at situations like this from both sides. As my title suggests, my primary concern is the national security of the United States. If Russia did annex Ukraine, would it pose any *more* of a threat to the U.S.? My answer is 'No'.

"The Russian Black Sea Fleet is already well-established in that area. Adding Odessa as another port would not make it more so. Russia's principal commodity export is oil. Having a Southern coastline on the Black Sea would make the Eastern Mediterranean more accessible. But the one place in the world which does not need more oil or petroleum products is the Eastern Mediterranean. Our Arab friends have had a corner on that market for longer than I have been alive."

With that, there were chuckles around the room from men who had fought in wars, some overt and some covert, which had allowed that eventuality to come to pass.

"*If* annexing Ukraine would make Russia more financially stable, or enhance their economy," resumed Winstead, "one could argue that the excess funds could be spent upon military hardware as well as research and development. But Russia does not seem to have any qualms over spending whatever money they need on the military at the expense of the quality of life for the average Russian citizen. Thus, I would say neither their economy nor their military strength would be enhanced by annexing Ukraine.

"The only downside I can see would be the establishing of a precedent. As with any dictatorial leader such as Napoleon or Hitler, Putin would take our failure to stop them at the Ukrainian border as a tacit exhibit of our indifference to further expansionism. And Putin has made no secret of his desire to have the Russian Federation replicate as much of the areal coverage of the Soviet Union as possible. That we *cannot* let happen," she concluded.

"Thank you, Ms. Winstead," said Jefferson. He turned to the Directors of the DIA, CIA, and NSA as if to inquire if they had anything to add. They each gently shook their heads.

"Okay, then," concluded Jefferson, "It seems as though we have a consensus. To date, we have stopped Russia and Putin in their tracks. Insanity is characterized as continuing to do the same thing while expecting a different result. Putin may be a megalomaniac, but he is not insane.

"When I speak with President Putin," said Jefferson in closing, "I will inform him that any further offensive overtures against Ukraine will meet with the same outcome. Thank you all for joining me at this ungodly hour. Good day." The President rose, as did everyone else, and they left.

Chapter Twenty-five

At 8:15 President Jefferson began making his way from the residence to the Oval Office. When he reached his office he took his seat at the *Resolute* desk and picked up the handset of one of the phones. He told the operator at the switchboard to get Ukrainian President Petro Poroshenko and to ring him back when she got through to him. At 8:37 the phone rang and the operator put Poroshenko on.

For the next ten minutes, Jefferson explained to the Ukrainian President just exactly how he was going to handle Putin and what he was going to say. Poroshenko thanked Jefferson profusely for all of the assistance the United States had provided his country and expressed his deepest regrets at the loss of six American lives. At the conclusion of the phone call, President Jefferson wished Poroshenko good luck in the first round of his nation's presidential election which would be taking place on March 31st, just a little more than three weeks away.

He bid Poroshenko farewell and hung up the phone. It was 8:52. In eight minutes the phone would ring again. Only this time it would be Vladimir Putin on the other end of the line. For those eight minutes, Jefferson made some last minute mental notes of exactly how he intended to handle the Russian President.

At 8:55 the Appointments Secretary showed the Russian interpreter from the State Department in. Jefferson pulled a chair up beside his and told him to take a seat. At precisely 9:00AM the phone rang for the second time that morning. Only this time the voice on the other end of the line would be that of one of only two people whose countries were aspiring world superpowers. Jefferson picked up the phone. Putin spoke first.

"President Jefferson, good morning," began Putin. "What may I do for you this fine day?"

Jefferson was momentarily thrown off balance by both the tone and innocence in Putin's voice and greeting. But he regained his bearings and went into attack mode.

"Look, Vladimir," he bellowed, "don't return my call on a morning like this as though this was some sort of courtesy call! When you invaded Ukraine, I told you exactly what you needed to do to avoid bloodshed. When you ignored me, I ordered my military to inflict the type of pain I had hoped we could avoid.

"Up until now the deaths, although regrettable, have, for the most part, been those of enemy combatants. We've lost six pilots. You've lost four aviators. And I've no idea how many of your ground troops have been killed. But, moving forward, this can only go one of two ways. The easy way or the hard way.

"The easy way is that you acknowledge that your invasion of Ukraine was a gross miscalculation on your part. That, in the future, there will be no more attempts to annex what you have characterized as a 'rogue republic'. Those Russian soldiers and aviators which have been taken captive by the Ukrainian military will be transported under heavily armed guard to the Russian embassy in Kiev by Ukrainian Army troops. They will, officially, be turned over to your acting ambassador there.

"Under heavy armed escort, you will be allowed to transport them back across the Russian border. Neither President Poroshenko nor I will ever expect to see their likes in Ukraine again. As for the four dead, their remains will be transported to a border crossing of our mutual satisfaction and handed over to your unarmed military medical staff for disposal as is your custom.

"The remnants of your destroyed aircraft, as well as those still able to fly but grounded due to the lack of usable runways, will become the property of Ukraine. The Ukrainians, with the assistance of American engineers and pilots, will closely examine both. Those which are salvageable will be restored. They, along with those which were not damaged, will become part of the Ukrainian Air Force.

American Air Force pilots and Weapons Systems

Officers will familiarize themselves with the Russian technologies embodied in your MiG-31s and Su-57s. Once that information has been gathered and transmitted back to the States, they will train the Ukrainian pilots and other aviation officers in the flight of the aircraft and the operation of their weapons.

"Finally, your Ambassador to the United Nations, Vasily Alekseevich Nebenzya, will offer a formal and very public apology to the Ukrainian Ambassador, Volodymyr Yelchenko, on the floor of the General Assembly for your incursion onto Ukrainian soil. Moreover, he will pledge that such an incursion will never again take place."

"I've heard enough!" blurted out Putin. "You destroy my ground weapons and kill my Army soldiers. You shoot down my aircraft and kill my aviators. Now, you want us to allow you to examine our military technologies so that you can either replicate them in American factories or devise countermeasures to render them useless. And, in an act of final humiliation, you want us to offer an apology to a representative of an illegitimate government which, for the time being, presumes to govern a territory which, by all rights, is an integral part of the Russian Federation."

"That's the *easy* way of bringing these hostilities to a conclusion," resumed Jefferson. "The alternative is the *hard* way. You'll like it even less. First, your soldiers and airmen will be imprisoned in the coldest, darkest military prison within the Ukrainian borders. Since Ukraine used to be a Soviet socialist republic, and you used to be a KGB agent, I'm sure you are familiar with the conditions in such a facility. You love to parade your sharply-dressed soldiers and roll your military hardware through Red Square in your May Day parades, only now you call them *Victory Day* parades. But we both know what little value you place on human life. Even the lives of those very soldiers. If you leave them to suffer in Ukrainian military prisons you will be exposed for the hypocrite you truly are.

"The aircraft will still belong to the Ukrainians after we have gleaned all of the military secrets and technologies they have to offer. That part of the offer will not change. But there's more.

"Ukraine is currently in the midst of a presidential campaign. President Poroshenko is but one of dozens of candidates. However, his biggest threat comes from a comedic actor by the name of Volodymyr Zelensky. Nonetheless, both have expressed the desire to bring Ukraine out of the shadow of Russia and into the 21st century. And both, during the course of their respective campaigns, have pledged to take Ukraine into both the European Union and NATO within their five-year terms of office.

"With respect to NATO, the United States pays by far the most and disproportionately large dues to maintain its viability in the face of the threat from the Eastern Bloc countries led by the Russian Federation. Thus, I personally have the leverage to facilitate whatever agenda I may want among our partners in the alliance. I am sure I could get Ukraine recognized as a member of NATO, your sworn enemy, in far less than five years.

"The United States is, of course, not a member of the EU. But most of my nation's staunchest allies are. With a well-placed kind word, and with the offer of a new, more favorable trade agreement, I'm sure I could get most of the EU's heads of state to welcome Ukraine into the club of first world, Western European nations within less than five years.

"Well, Vladimir, the choice is yours. We can do this the easy way or the hard way. Oh, and there's one more way, but I think you'll like it even less than the previous two. Along with some of the Baltic States which were once part of the Warsaw Pact, many of your so-called allies have somewhat unreliable diplomatic relationships with Russia. They could waiver. Moreover, I could go out of my way to court some heads of state such as President Erdoğan of Turkey. He saved you from the ravages of our F-22 *Raptors* this time around. He may not be so compliant next time."

"I will not be threatened!" yelled Putin in response. "I will not be blackmailed! This is not the way nations conduct diplomacy." The next thing Jefferson heard was a click, a period of silence, and then a dial tone. Putin had hung up.

Chapter Twenty-six

After he had dismissed the interpreter, President Jefferson got on the phone to his Secretary of State.

"Charles, John Jefferson here," he started. "I just had a somewhat acrimonious telephone conference with President Putin. He didn't like any of the ways I proposed for bringing his country's invasion of Ukraine to an end." For the next ten minutes, Secretary Wainwright wrote furiously as Jefferson dictated the terms of the first two options which the President had offered Putin.

"It is now ten o'clock. The first thing I want you to do is call Ambassador Anatoly Antonov at the Russian Embassy out on Wisconsin Avenue in Georgetown. Tell him that I will be expecting him in my office promptly at 1:00PM. Next, I want you to have the terms for the cessation of hostilities in Ukraine which I enumerated for you reduced to writing and composed as a three-party peace treaty among Ukraine, the Russian Federation, and the United States. I also want both the easy and hard options formatted as bulleted lists. And, third, I want you to join me for lunch in the residence at Noon so that we can work out the details of our joint meeting with the ambassador this afternoon."

"I'll be there at Noon with the documents you

requested," said the former admiral. It made him proud to be the head of the State Department under a president who knew what he wanted and would go to any lengths to extract compliance from our adversaries. "This should make for quite an interesting afternoon and next few days," said Wainwright. "If I might add, Sir, I would suggest imposing a deadline for the signing of a treaty by, say, 3:00PM on Friday. Then we can execute a Friday afternoon document dump which has become such a custom in Washington. No one much follows the news on the weekend, and by Monday morning it is virtually certain that some more recent event will be leading the news on the network shows at sunrise."

"Excellent idea, Charles," responded Jefferson. "When we meet with Antonov, I don't plan to make any undue or explicit threats. I want to let him, Foreign Minister Lavrov, and Putin go through the exercise of trying to read between the lines. What they imagine will no doubt be more severe than anything I would be willing to commit to writing."

"Good thinking, Mister President," said Wainwright.

"Okay, then," concluded Jefferson. "I'll see you at Noon."

* * *

Lunch that day for the President and his Secretary of

State consisted of some intense and highly animated exchanges as they gamed out the potential responses they might expect from the leader of the Russian Federation. In each case, they devised what they deemed would be an appropriate response. They ranged from cordial to bellicose.

Shortly before 1:00PM, the two men strode through the halls of the White House to the Oval Office. When they got there, they had a brief discussion as to whether the President should be seated behind the *Resolute* desk or in the lounge chair at the head of the ornate glass-topped coffee table in the sitting area for the meeting. The conclusion incorporated both. When the ambassador arrived, Jefferson would be at his desk, thereby forcing the ambassador to make the effort to formally present himself to the President while standing across the desk from him. Only then would Jefferson invite him to take a seat at the far end of the leather couch positioned on the long side of the coffee table. Wainwright would sit at the near end at the President's left hand. The two-to-one American advantage would be self-evident. There would be no coffee or cookies this day.

At 1:00PM, two plain-clothed Secret Service agents with their sidearms concealed but prominently bulging beneath their suit coats knocked on the door and then escorted Russian Ambassador Antonov into the Oval Office. He crossed the powder-blue rug bearing the seal of the President of the United States and took his respectful position across the desk from the seated President. Only then did Jefferson rise and extend his hand in a feigned gesture of friendship.

Jefferson motioned for Antonov to move to the sitting area. The President and Secretary Wainwright took their seats first, ensuring that Antonov would end up on the far end of the couch setting up an adversarial dynamic. Then Jefferson prepared to move in for the kill.

"Ambassador Antonov," began the President, "The subject for today is Ukraine. Four hours ago I had a rather unpleasant telephone call with your Mister Putin."

"So I have been told," said the ambassador.

"Thus far the United States and the Russian Federation have experienced two rounds of skirmishes both on the ground and in the air above Ukrainian soil. These events were not like the frequent encounters between Russian and American aircraft where one flies dangerously close to the other in an attempt to make their adversary change course or cease their mission to invade the other's airspace.

"Weapons have been fired and combatants on both sides have been killed. Aircraft have been shot down and tanks have been destroyed. We are, Mister Ambassador, perilously close to an all-out war over the territorial integrity and independence of Ukraine.

"The United States has no desire to fire a single additional round. We simply wish to have Ukraine left in peace. The first of the two pages which Secretary Wainwright has handed you lists the terms whereby we can bring this episode to a conclusion under the most humane manner of conduct. The second page enumerates the consequences if President Putin refuses to agree to the terms on the first. As you review them I am sure that you would agree with me that the terms on the first page are far preferable to those on the second."

"I can see the stark contrast, President Jefferson," said Ambassador Antonov, "But you clearly know that I am not empowered to consent to any terms. I am but a representative of my superiors, Foreign Minister Lavrov and President Putin. Only they, in collaboration, can commit the Russian Federation to such a course of action."

"I am well aware of that, Mister Ambassador," replied Jefferson. "What Secretary Wainwright is now handing you is a thumb drive. On it are three document files. The first is a copy of the bulleted list of terms for a civilized cessation of the hostilities. The second is a list of the consequences should the terms on the first list not be agreed to.

"The third document is by far the most important. It is, for all intents and purposes, a tripartite peace treaty. It is write-protected with the exception of three pairs of blanks wherein each party may insert a signature and date. No changes of a single letter of the text may be made.

"I want you to return to your embassy and have one of your computer-literate staff members transmit the files on that thumb drive to Foreign Minister Lavrov in Moscow. Explain to him that he is to review the files and then present them as documents to your President Putin. Mister Putin is to consider them thoughtfully.

"When your President is convinced that the peace treaty is the only viable alternative, he is to digitally sign and date it and have it sent to Secretary Wainwright's office. When we are satisfied that the text has not been tampered with, I will sign and date it. Finally, we will send it to President Poroshenko in Kiev to have it signed and dated as it is his nation's future to which both your president and I will be committing ourselves.

"It is now 1:30PM Washington time, 9:30PM Moscow time. You should be able to have the contents of the thumb drive in the hands of Minister Lavrov by midnight tonight. Make sure to have one of your staff call his residence and alert him that these documents are on their way. Time is of the essence.

"When Minister Lavrov has convinced himself that signing the treaty is the only rational course of action, he is to have the documents delivered to President Putin regardless of the time of day or night. He may wish to do so himself so that he can confer with Mister Putin in person. Once the treaty has been signed and dated, have it transmitted to Secretary Wainwright. The deadline is 3:00PM Washington time on Friday,"

"But President Jefferson," blurted out a clearly distressed Ambassador Antonov, "that is barely 48 hours. Such a momentous decision will surely take more time to make. President Putin may solicit the input of the country's military leadership or members of his diplomatic corps. Simply getting them all to Moscow and conducting such meetings could well take more than 48 hours in themselves."

"The decision for President Putin is simple," replied President Jefferson. "It should take little or no thought on either Minister Lavrov's or Mister Putin's part. I can assure you in no uncertain terms that the alternative is not an eventuality that Russia wants to pursue."

"Just what, exactly, would that alternative consist of?" asked Antonov.

"That, Mister Ambassador, is not something of which I will speak," responded Jefferson. "All I can say is that it is not something that you, Minister Lavrov, President Putin, or the Russian people want to find out."

"But how can I offer Foreign Minister Lavrov my

counsel if I cannot tell him what the alternatives are?" inquired the ambassador.

"Look at my face, Ambassador Antonov," answered the President. "Listen to the tone of my voice. Is there any doubt in your mind that I am sincere in my desire to see this episode in our countries' history draw to a close? Moreover, do you have any doubt that I will do whatever it takes to make it so?

"Don't think for a minute that I will not make the conciliatory nature of my nation's offer to spare any further bloodshed known throughout the world's diplomatic circles. No one will want to see the alternative. And if you refuse our offer you may well find that your allies, as well as your enemies, will be reluctant to negotiate with you in the future."

"This meeting is now over," concluded President Jefferson. He called out to the two Secret Service agents stationed just outside the door to the Oval Office to come in. "Gentlemen," he said, "would you kindly escort Ambassador Antonov out to his awaiting limousine? He has a lot of work to do and little time in which to do it."

The two agents waited as Antonov rose from the couch, shoved the thumb drive into his pocket, and joined them at the door. When the three had exited the Oval Office, Jefferson and Wainwright exchanged self-satisfied smiles.

Chapter Twenty-seven

Russian Ambassador Anatoly Antonov's limousine pulled out of West Executive Avenue onto Pennsylvania Avenue and turned West-Northwest to head back to his embassy. After crossing the bridge over Rock Creek, the route took a slight turn to the left as it became "M" Street in Georgetown. Just a few blocks further on, the vehicle turned right onto Wisconsin Avenue.

Climbing Wisconsin Avenue Northward, the limo turned left when it reached the driveway to the 12.5-acre Russian Embassy compound and drove up the hill which, until 1967, had housed the Mt. Alto Veterans Hospital. When the vehicle reached the building's entrance, Antonov disembarked and made his way to his office as quickly as possible. Once seated behind his desk, he called the Information Technology (IT) office and told the head of IT to report to his office immediately. It was now 9:50PM Moscow time.

When he arrived, the ambassador told the techie that the thumb drive he was handing him had three critical files on it. Those files were to be transmitted to the office of Prime Minister Sergey Lavrov in Moscow immediately. The ambassador was informed that, before the files could be allowed to be transmitted or the thumb drive even plugged into a computer attached to the secure Russian Internet network, the device would have to be scanned for malicious software.

Ambassador Antonov became visibly agitated, but he knew that the computer expert knew his job and that he was absolutely right about scanning the device. If it did contain malware, connecting it to the network could compromise the system and give the Americans access to Russia's most closely held secrets. As it turned out, the thumb drive was clean.

As soon as he had handed over the thumb drive, Ambassador Antonov had made two phone calls. The first was to the night watch officer in the offices of the Foreign Minister in the Ministry of Foreign Affairs building at 32/34 Smolenskaya-Sennaya Square in Moscow. He told him that three critical classified files were being transmitted to the Foreign Minister's personal computer.

Antonov instructed the watch officer that, when they were received, two hard copies of each of the three documents were to be printed out and two CDs of the three files made. They were then to be immediately hand delivered to the residence of Foreign Minister Lavrov on the outskirts of Moscow by an armed foreign ministry courier who was to then await further orders from the minister. It was quite possible that he would have to either drive or accompany the minister to the Kremlin.

Ambassador Antonov's second phone call was made directly to Foreign Minister Lavrov himself on his secure residential line. The ambassador heard a series of alternating tones while the two secure comms devices synched up. When the phone was finally answered, all he heard was "Lavrov". It was 10:13PM and the Foreign Minister had already gone to bed for the night and fallen asleep.

"Foreign Minister Lavrov," began the ambassador, "It is Anatoly Antonov. I apologize for calling you at such a late hour, but this is an emergency."

"Yes, yes, Antonov," Lavrov grumbled, "What is it?"

"I have just come from the office of the President of the United States," resumed Antonov. "There I met with him and Secretary of State Wainwright. As you know, Jefferson spoke with President Putin earlier today. I was given three documents in digital file format which I was instructed to transmit to you. They should be on their way to your office at the Ministry momentarily.

"The three documents are a list of demands by the United States for a cessation of their military intervention in the conflict between us and Ukraine, a list of the consequences if the terms of the first document are not met, and a peace treaty which their Department of State has prepared to be signed by President Jefferson, President

Poroshenko, and President Putin."

"What arrogance!" exclaimed Lavrov. "Who are they to dictate to us?"

"I am only the messenger, Sir," replied Antonov timidly. "I spoke with the night watch officer at the Ministry and informed him that the three files were being transmitted to your personal computer in your office over our secure network. I instructed him to make two hard copies of each and to make two CDs, each containing all three documents. When he has done that, he will give them to a courier who will hand deliver them to your residence. From that point on, what you choose to do with them is clearly at your discretion."

"You did the right thing, Antonov," replied Lavrov. "I will take this matter from here. You are to have no further contact with President Jefferson or Secretary Wainwright without first speaking with me. Is that clear?"

"Very clear, Mister Minister," answered Antonov.

"All right then, Anatoly," said Lavrov, "When I have reviewed the documents I will decide what further steps we may have to take."

"There is one more thing, Minister Lavrov," uttered Antonov reluctantly.

"What is is, Antonov?" asked Lavrov.

"President Jefferson made it abundantly clear that the deadline for his receiving a file containing the peace treaty signed by President Putin is 3:00PM Washington time on Friday. If he does not have it by then, we are to expect, at a minimum, the consequences enumerated in the second document."

"That is less than two full days from now!" screamed Lavrov. "Does he not understand that ours is a tremendous bureaucracy? How are we to consult with our military, legislative, and party leadership within that short amount of time to try and reach some sort of consensus? It cannot be done."

"I am merely relaying his message, Foreign Minister," answered Antonov. "I was not given any say in the matter, nor was I allowed to respond. I am sure that you and President Putin will do the correct thing."

"I can assure you we will," replied Lavrov. "Now I must go. I have much to do. Goodbye, Anatoly." And, with that, Lavrov hung up.

* * *

It was shortly after midnight when the courier from

the Ministry of Foreign Affairs arrived at the residence of Foreign Minister Lavrov with the six documents and two CDs. Lavrov directed the courier to the kitchen and told him to help himself to a cup of coffee from the pot which the housekeeper kept going all night. Then Lavrov made his way to the study where he turned on a reading lamp and took a seat in an overstuffed leather chair to read for himself the documents which Ambassador Antonov had described.

When he had finished, it was clearly evident to him that he must share the contents of the documents with President Putin at the earliest possible opportunity. It was, by then, 12:40 in the morning. Although he was reluctant to do so, he prepared to call the president. The hour was unfortunate, but it would not be the first time he had awakened Vladimir Putin in the middle of the night.

"President Putin," began Lavrov when the president had answered his phone, "I regret the late hour for this call, but circumstances have arisen of which I thought you should be immediately informed. This afternoon in Washington, our Ambassador Anatoly Antonov was summoned to the White House to meet with the president and Secretary of State Wainwright. He was given crucial documents which he was instructed were to be immediately be shared with me.

"These documents were given to him in digital format and they were transmitted to my office. The night watch officer had them printed out as well as burned onto CDs and hand-delivered to me here at home. I have read them and believe that you should read them at the earliest possible moment.

"What is it about these documents that make it so urgent that I read them?" asked Putin.

"They lay out the terms for the United States to cease its intervention in our ongoing hostilities with Ukraine and are accompanied by what can only be characterized as a peace treaty. It must be signed by you, President Jefferson, and President Poroshenko," said Lavrov hesitantly.

"I heard all of this before from President Jefferson himself when he and I spoke on the telephone this afternoon," answered Putin, clearly growing frustrated.

"Yes, Mister President, I understand that," replied Lavrov, "but there is now a provision attached which was not part of your discussion with Jefferson. He told Antonov that the deadline for his receiving a digitally-signed copy of the treaty was 3:00PM Washington time on Friday, 11:00PM Moscow time. He said that if he did not have an executed document in hand by then, the United States would begin to carry out the actions which he enumerated in his list of consequences for non-compliance."

So, he is once again making with the ultimatum which he believes he can impose upon us," said Putin, half as a question and half as a statement. "Since I do not respond to ultimatums from either at home or abroad, this can wait. Be in my office with the documents at 10:00AM in the morning and we shall review them together. Then I will decide what our next course of action will be."

"But, Sir," responded Lavrov, "that's more than nine hours from now. We are running out of time."

"What I am running out of," bellowed Putin, "is patience with your subservient attitude toward this cowboy Jefferson. I will not be dictated to by some former college football player from Notre Dame. And I will not tolerate the threats which he made to me over the phone yesterday afternoon. We have a number of situations here at home, some economic, some political, and some military, which must be considered. Any sign of weakness on my part can jeopardize both my future and Russia's. 10:00AM this morning, Sergey."

"Yes, Mister President," replied Lavrov, and he hung up the phone. But Putin was not now done for the night. He placed a series of phone calls. The first was to the adjutant for the Marshal of the Russian Federation, General Igor Sergeyev. The next call was to Dmitry Medvedev, Prime Minister and Chairman of the Government of the Russian Federation. The third was to Igor Sechin, senior, and perhaps wealthiest, among the influential Russian oligarchs.

Chapter Twenty-eight

The future of Ukraine, the continued involvement of the United States in the military encounters there, and, most directly, the political, economic, and military stability of the Russian Federation all rested in the hands of one man: Vladimir Vladimirovich Putin. To the Russians, Putin represented the past glories and ultimate destiny of Mother Russia. To the rest of the world, he was a narcissistic, megalomaniacal dictator.

The 66-year-old President of the Russian Federation was born and raised in St. Petersburg. After graduating from Leningrad State University in 1975, he spent a 16-year career as a foreign intelligence officer for the KGB. He entered politics in St. Petersburg in 1991.

In 1996, Putin moved to Moscow and went into government service under Boris Yeltsin. On December 31, 1999, he ascended to the position of Acting President when Yeltsin resigned. Beginning in 2000, he was elected to two four-year terms as President of the Russian Federation. Because of Russia's term limits, he could not run for a third consecutive term. Dmitry Medvedev succeeded him in a placeholder role as president for one four-year term.

In 2012, Putin was elected to a six-year term as returning President earning 64% of the vote, and, in 2018, he was re-elected for a second six-year term with 76% of the vote.

Putin is very image-conscious and he manages every aspect of that image in minute detail. His persona is one which mirrors the attributes and strengths which Russians admire and which they attribute to their homeland. Putin can frequently be seen in widely-distributed film clips fishing, hunting, or riding bare-chested on a powerful horse.

His management style was authoritarian, much of which, in all likelihood, grew out of his 16 years with the KGB. To deal with the current crisis in Ukraine, he would consult military leaders, legislative and party leaders, and the cream of the oligarchy, all in that order. But first, he would meet with Foreign Minister Lavrov.

The minister arrived at Putin's Kremlin outer office promptly at 10:00AM. He was shown into Putin's palatial inner office where he was told to take a seat. Just to exhibit who was in control, Putin arrived 15 minutes later.

"So, Sergey, what do you think of our President Jefferson's ultimatum?" asked Putin with no preliminary greeting.

"I find it very disconcerting, Mister President," replied Lavrov. "If we were to sign this document, it would definitely diminish Russia in the eyes of the world and you in the eyes of the Russian people. It is tantamount to a statement of surrender rather than a template for peace."

"I quite agree," said Putin. "Jefferson is trying to make us look like dogs running home with our tails tucked between our legs. The Russian people will not stand for it, and neither will I."

"What alternative do you have in mind?" asked Lavrov. "His list of consequences should we not do as he has directed is quite problematic. There is, after all, the diplomatic, political, and economic fallout to consider.

"In terms of the diplomatic implications, Ukraine is pushing for a membership vote by NATO not later than 2024. Jefferson gives every indication that he could get that date moved up. We are nearly encompassed by NATO members on our Western border. Ukraine would extend that containment to the South as well. And, as much as we protest, the head of the European Union continues to say that Ukraine represents an integral part of Europe."

"This is all just so much talk," said Putin.

"It may be talk," replied Lavrov with some hesitation, "but people are listening. Two of the three top tier candidates in the Ukrainian presidential election 24 days hence have committed to joining NATO. The same goes for the EU. The third candidate probably agrees as well. With

NATO comes the Article V protection of the United States and with the EU comes a more vibrant economy. Are you certain we can withstand both?" inquired Lavrov.

"We must," said Putin. "It is what our people expect of us. If we are to return Russia to its glorious status as a fearsome bear on Europe's Eastern border, we cannot be seen shrinking from an American threat."

"But, Sir," said Lavrov, "It is more than our reputation at stake. Hundreds of Russian soldiers have been killed. Our foray into Ukraine has proven costly in both Russian blood and treasure. Support among the people on the street has waned. They won't see it as surrender. They will see it as self-preservation."

"To Hell with the man in the street," replied Putin. "I still have the power to strike fear in their hearts when need be. Once our economy rebounds, they will thank me for standing up to the Americans."

"Sir, as you well know," said Lavrov, "the trade sanctions imposed upon us by the Americans and Europeans in the face of our re-annexing Crimea five years ago are weighing heavily upon our economy. Moreover, the price of oil, our only exportable commodity, has, on several occasions, dropped to all-time lows.

"President Jefferson still maintains close ties with the

Saudis and other Middle Eastern oil-producing nations. All he need do is ask and they will increase their oil production which will result in lower prices for petroleum-based products and increase out trade deficits even further."

"You're beginning to sound like Jefferson himself," bellowed Putin. "Who's side are you on? Perhaps your 15 years at the Ministry of Foreign Affairs has made you more concerned with what others think of Russia than what we think of ourselves."

"That will be all, Sergey," exclaimed the President. "You are excused."

* * *

President Putin's next meeting was scheduled to begin at 11:30. It would include the military leaders with whom he met in advance of Russia's invasion of Ukraine. When they arrived at the Kremlin from around Moscow, they convened in the same conference room as previously. Only this time the subject would not be the battle plan for the occupation of Ukraine but rather the abject failure of the Russian forces in the face of the response which the American forces had posed at the request of the Ukrainian president.

Once again around the conference table were Sergey Shoygu, General of the Army, General Andrey Yudin,

Marshal of Aviation, Admiral Vladimir Korolyov, Admiral of the Fleet, and, finally, General Igor Sergeyev, Marshal of the Russian Federation. The only participant from the previous meeting who was not at the table was Sergey Lavrov with whom the Russian president had already dealt. Putin convened the meeting with a dressing down of his entire military establishment.

"Gentlemen," began Putin, "When last we met you all presented me with a straightforward plan which, at its conclusion, was to have resulted in the occupation of Ukraine in preparation for its annexation as part of the Russian Federation. General Shoygu, your Army troops were to be the vanguard for the invasion, creating positions in four critical locations from which to establish hegemony across the whole of Ukraine. In anticipation of President Poroshenko's solicitation of American assistance, these encampments were to be placed in such a way that the enemy pilots would not dare bomb them for fear of killing hundreds, if not thousands, of civilians as well as destroying key infrastructure facilities as well as revered religious sites. What went wrong?"

"Mister President," answered General Shoygu, "We executed our plan exactly as it was presented to you. When our tanks rolled across the border, they met with little, if any resistance. Each element made the fastest headway possible to their destinations. They established positions in Kiev, Kharkiv, and Odessa. The fourth element set up our command and control center in a city in central Ukraine.

In each case, the soldiers established their positions in close proximity to targets which we were certain that the Americans would not attack for fear of killing Ukrainians or crippling their infrastructure. Those sites included encampments adjacent to government buildings, power plants, and subway stations, as well as apartment buildings and schools. We believed ourselves to be immune from aerial attack by enemy aircraft because the American people and the world community would not tolerate the mass execution of innocent men, women, and children as well as those facilities upon which the Ukrainians depend to support their daily way of life. In Kharkiv specifically, we placed our tanks, artillery, and mobile SAM launchers adjacent to four historically significant religious structures; an Orthodox cathedral, a Roman Catholic cathedral, a synagogue, and a mosque.

"However, unbeknownst to us, the Americans had developed a bomb which, while destroying its target, did not send shrapnel flying in all directions to cut down civilians or devastate buildings. Its housing simply disintegrated; vaporized if you will. They were free to fire at will at our military vehicles without fear of killing Ukrainians or inflicting damage on their buildings. This is why they were so successful. And when their aircrafts' allotment of bombs was exhausted, they each made one more pass to strafe the surviving soldiers on the ground with their rotary cannons."

"How is it that our military intelligence services were unaware of the existence of such bombs?" asked an exasperated Putin.

"Apparently these weapons were developed in a classified facility somewhere in their California. Not only will the housing vaporize upon the warhead's detonation, but the pilot may actually adjust the power of the bomb for the specific target while en route from its base to its destination. As we had expected, the vast number of American aircraft came from the NATO base at Aviano, Italy. The remainder came from an American aircraft carrier in the Black Sea."

"That leads me to my next question," interrupted Putin. "Admiral Korolyov, exactly what role did the Russian Navy play in this debacle?"

"Sir," answered the admiral, "the role of the Black Sea Fleet was to cordon off the Southern coastline of Ukraine to prevent enemy troops from using it put troops on the ground. The American navy's ships were well into international waters and they posed no immediate threat to our troops in Odessa. In accordance with maritime rules, we did not attack them in international waters, nor did they attack us. Ultimately, the only action those ships took was to fire blindly upon American stealth fighters as they returned to their aircraft carrier after their attacks on our weapons and troops in Ukraine."

"That brings me to you, General Yudin," said Putin. "As we expected, this conflict was ultimately an air war. It was my understanding that our aircraft were equivalent, if not superior, to anything the Americans could put in the air above Ukraine. Explain to me, in detail, just what exactly went wrong."

"At first," responded Yudin timidly, "everything went as planned. We had our MiG-31s flying throughout Ukrainian airspace to create a no-fly zone. They are far faster and equally as maneuverable as the American F-16s. However, we had not anticipated that their Air force would introduce two *Lancer* bombers from as far away as Qatar.

"We had our MiG-31s not in the air at an airport for refueling and maintenance. There, also, were our Su-57s in the event they would be needed for high-speed, high-powered aerial combat. On the two occasions when the *Lancers* entered Ukrainian airspace, they flew to the airport where the out-of-service MiG-31s and Su-57s were lined up on the taxiways awaiting a call to scramble. Each time they overflew Ukraine they not only destroyed a number of aircraft on the ground, but they severely damaged the runways so that no surviving aircraft could take off.

"But it was my understanding that not only our aircraft but our pilots were superior to theirs," interjected Putin. "Was I misinformed?"

"No, Sir," replied Yudin. "But they have an extraordinary program which helps prepare their pilots to deal with any of our aerial tactics. It is known as Exercise Red Flag. It is a two-week advanced aerial combat training school designed exclusively for the purpose of preparing American pilots from their Air Force, Navy, and Marine Corps to respond and react to Russian aerial combat tactics.

"They use an 'aggressor flight' of aircraft comparable to ours flown by American pilots using our own aerial combat tactics to attack the trainee pilots' aircraft. Thus, they learn how to avoid the mistakes which an average pilot might make in combat against us as well as to respond in such a way as to gain the upper hand."

"And just how would they know our aerial combat tactics?" asked a clearly agitated Putin.

"Not only have they observed our pilot training using their reconnaissance capabilities, Sir, but they have interrogated Russian pilots who have defected," answered Yudin. There is one more thing, Sir."

"And what might that be, General Yudin?" asked Putin.

"Until the final two aerial encounters," replied Yudin, "with the exception of the two *Lancer* bombers, all of the enemy aircraft were American F-16s or F-18s. In the last two, the F-18s were replaced with F-35Cs, supersonic, stealth, multirole fighters flying off the deck of the American aircraft carrier in the Black Sea. The F-35Cs were on board the *Truman*, but they had not been certified as ready for combat by the U.S. Navy until last week. Their stealth characteristics enabled them to all but evade detection by either our MiG-31s or mobile SAM launchers. Our pilots fought valiantly, but the Americans ultimately gained the upper hand. If we should engage in any further aerial combat, I fear the outcome may be disastrous."

"That will be enough, Yudin," said President Putin.

"So, General Sergeyev, I turn to you as Marshal of the Russian Federation. What are we to do about Ukraine? Our Army can overwhelm the Ukrainian army at will and go anywhere within the country's borders they wish. But, it seems, with the assistance of the American Air Force and Navy aircraft, the Ukrainians can ultimately inflict unsustainable damage on our weapons and troops. Our navy could prevent an American land invasion, but that does not seem to be their intent."

"Mister President," Sergeyev responded in heavily nuanced tones, "Russia's Army troops are as good as any in the world. But, due to the limitations on expenditures to repair and replace our equipment, we cannot either inflict the level of damage we would wish or defend ourselves against a better-equipped adversary. Our Navy fleet is old and its weaponry becoming outmoded. Only our submarine fleet is state-of-the-art, but they are, for the most part, in the Arctic or North Atlantic. Even so, it does not seem that this battle is to be won or lost at sea.

"Now, as for our Air Force, our pilots are the best-trained in the world and, to put it bluntly, far more daring than their American counterparts. Moreover, our aircraft are every bit as good as theirs. The problem is the American economy. Our supply of aircraft is limited. Theirs is not. In an air war of attrition, the Americans will win. I can only recommend that we cease this incursion before it escalates beyond the borders of Ukraine onto the soil of one or more nations who are members of NATO."

"You know I respect your opinion, Igor," said Putin reluctantly. "But you are, at heart, a soldier, not a politician. There are other's opinions which I must solicit before I make a decision as to how the Russian Federation is to proceed in this matter.

"I will keep in mind what you and your commanders have said here today. This afternoon I will be meeting with the other members of the Security Council. Finally, I shall be dining with a group of the nation's prominent opinion leaders in an attempt to take the pulse of the country. When I have decided what course of action we will take, I will inform you immediately. Thank you for your candid input."

Chapter Twenty-nine

President Putin's next meeting was at 2:00PM in the same conference room. This one was to be with the legislative and party leaders of the nation. Collectively they were known as the Security Council. It was composed of twelve permanent members who held positions within the government or the party and twenty-six who represented various political subdivisions within the Russian Federation. For the purpose of this meeting, only permanent members would be in attendance. Putin was one, as was Lavrov. But Lavrov had already been consulted and dismissed, so there would be only Putin and the other ten.

In terms of authority, the second most powerful administration member was Dmitry Medvedev whose formal title was Chairman of the Government but who was always referred to simply as Prime Minister. After him came, in order, Manager of the Presidential Administration, Chairwoman of the Federation Council of the Federal Assembly, Chairman of the State Duma of the Federal Assembly, Minister for Defense, Minister for Internal Affairs, Director of the Federal Security Service (FSB, the successor to the KGB), Director of the Foreign Intelligence Service, Director of the Federal National Guard Troops Service, and the Secretary of the Security Council. Putin started off the discussion.

"Good afternoon, Lady and Gentlemen," the President intoned. "I want to thank all of you for making time in your busy schedules to join me here today. As you will have noticed, Minister Lavrov is not present. He and I have already spoken. And just a short while ago, I met with the leadership of our military. The subject of the meeting is our military intervention in Ukraine.

"The military does the fighting and dying, but the future of Mother Russia is entrusted to us. The military leaders seemed to believe that it was sheer folly to continue in our attempts to occupy Ukraine as a precursor to annexing it as just another republic in the Russian Federation. But it has historical, geographic, and economic significance.

"Due to the trade sanctions which have been imposed upon us by the West as retaliation for our annexation of Crimea five years ago, our economy is stagnating. Moreover, the price of crude oil is uncharacteristically low, thus reducing the value of our sole export commodity save uranium. The warm water ports along the Black Sea coastline in Ukraine provide more easy access to the Mediterranean and its markets than do any others available to us.

"Finally, outside the realm of economics, we must take into consideration the reality that, on the world stage, to let it appear that Ukraine, with the overwhelming assistance of the United States, was able to deter our simply occupying and annexing their land mass on our very doorstep is highly humiliating. We are a world superpower with a nuclear arsenal second only to that of the Americans. We can strike and obliterate the capital of any nation in the world with our aircraft and missiles. We cannot let the situation as it stands persist. We must, in my opinion, press the issue and take the battle to the Ukrainians and, if necessary, the Americans."

Putin then turned to Sergei Shoigu, the Minister for Defense. "Tell me, Sergei," asked the President, "what are you hearing in the halls of your offices at Znamenka 19?" referring to the address of the main office building of the Ministry for Defense. There was a protracted period of silence before Shoigu began to speak.

"Mister President," he began, "we lost a tremendous number of officers and men in the American air attacks on our four Army positions in Ukraine. Moreover, we lost two aircrews and others are being held captive. And that is before one takes into consideration the destruction of tanks, artillery, mobile SAM launchers, and MiG-31s.

"Morale is, at best, poor. I know it is your job to make policy decisions and the military's job to enact those policies which must be carried out by force, but the fighting men do not understand why it is that we must prosecute a *de facto* war on Ukraine. I have men in my services who were born in Ukraine or whose family or ancestors are, or were, Ukrainian. In addition, as you well know, there are many ethnic Russians who currently reside in Ukraine. Not all of them support the pro-Russian rebels. We are losing equipment at an alarming rate. But what I am sincerely concerned about is that we may soon begin to lose the will of our fighting men."

"That is what your officers are for!" exclaimed Putin.

"With all due respect, President Putin," replied Shoigu, "many of my officers are of Ukrainian descent. Their hearts are not in this battle. And if their hearts are not in it, there is little hope of them exhorting their troops on to victory. My recommendation is that we cease this folly before we lose any more men *or* machines."

"This cannot be," bemoaned Putin. "Soldiers wage war with their hearts. Those of us in this room are entrusted with the awesome responsibility of waging war with our heads. It is the future and the greater glory of the homeland which is at stake. Ukraine was once an integral part of the Soviet Union. It must once again become a vital component of the Russian Federation."

"What say you?" asked Putin, turning to Valentina Matviyenko, a fellow native of St. Petersburg and Chairwoman of the Federation Council of the Federal Assembly, the upper house of the Russian legislature. She was the third most powerful member of the Russian government.

"What I hear on the floor of the Federation Council is dissent bordering on desertion," said Matviyenko. "This council has eighteen non-permanent members. And each of those members has constituents, constituents who reside in our federal districts and oblasts. It is to them that those members must answer. And it is the conduct of the constituents which is bordering on unrest.

"It should not be surprising that there is unrest on the streets of Ukraine which is under armed attack by the Russian Federation," concluded the chairwoman, "but if we begin to see unrest on the streets of the Federation itself, the battle will be lost at home as well as across the border in Ukraine."

"I cannot believe what I am hearing," said Putin. "Prime Minister Medvedev, help me out here. Tell me truthfully, are we governing the masses or are the masses governing us?" It only took moments for Dmitry Medvedev, the second most powerful member of the Russian government, to respond.

"Mister President," said Medvedev, "there are three audiences to this conflict. The first is the Russian people. They must see that, in the end, there is benefit to the Russian Federation for conducting this occupation and annexation if they are to support it. The second audience is the rest of the world, most importantly those nations which were once

Warsaw Pact countries or other lands within the Soviet Union's sphere of influence. And the third is the Ukrainians themselves.

"The Russian people are tired of war or the threat of war. For nearly five decades they lived under the threat of nuclear annihilation during the Cold War. And that does not even take into consideration our military adventurism in Afghanistan. We were told that NATO and, in particular, the United States were our enemy. Now they see the Americans coming to the aid of one of the former republics of the Soviet Union. And Ukraine is not even a member of NATO to whose aid the U.S. would be compelled to contribute under the provisions of Article V. They wonder if they were lied to for those five decades.

"Within the diplomatic community, our actions are seen as unacceptable. Following the collapse of the Soviet Union, Ukraine was acknowledged the world over as an independent and sovereign nation with well-defined borders and an internationally-recognized governing body. It occupies a seat at the United Nations. And its president has explicitly stated that he expects Ukraine to become a member of both the European Union and NATO by 2024. Both of those organizations have shown every indication that they welcome and support that ambition.

"And then there are the Ukrainians themselves. Could they possibly fend off an armed invasion by Russia on their own? Of course not. They do not possess the manpower, and their antiquated military equipment is little more than that which was ceded to them by us following the collapse of the Soviet Union. It is virtually all in either poor repair or inoperable. Their economy is such that they cannot afford to replace it. That is why Poroshenko called upon the United States which still recognizes Russia as their most formidable military adversary.

"Some American politicians have ridiculed those who do not see China as their most fearsome enemy. But it is those who do not recognize Russia's military might who have been shown to be the fools. And the Americans have the Atlantic and Pacific Oceans as a buffer between themselves and the Russian Federation. The European nations do not possess such a luxury. They hate us because they fear us. And that fear is well-placed. But if you poke them or one of their allies one too many times, they may poke back.

"When we think of warfare, we usually think of guns and bullets. But there is economic warfare as well. The sanctions imposed upon us by the West for the re-annexation of Crimea has already taken its toll.

"If we persist in our campaign in Ukraine, further sanctions could well cripple our economy. And the Americans can collude with the nations of OPEC to flood the world markets with crude oil. Should that happen, where would Russia look to generate the capital necessary to run the largest country in the world? With more than 10% of the Earth's total land mass, our Asian portion makes us the largest country in Asia and our European portion makes us the largest country in Europe. How does one run such a country with fewer and fewer trading partners?

"Our invasion of Ukraine has either alienated those nations who still trade with us or given them pause as to the wisdom of doing so. If they do, they risk becoming pariahs among the community of nations. And no nation can afford to risk having Russia as its only trading partner

"Finally, the last audience is the Ukrainians themselves. They are a proud people with a long history. Three-quarters of the country's population is made up of ethnic Ukrainians. It is true that roughly one-fifth of their population are ethnic Russians. But it would be a grievous and foolhardy error to trust that they all support the pro-Russian rebels within their borders. If they wanted to be citizens of Russia, they need only cross over the border. The fact that they have not is indicative of their desire to remain Ukrainian citizens.

"In conclusion," wound down Medvedev, "I can only counsel you in the strongest of terms to cease this pursuit of annexing Ukraine. To continue to do so will only antagonize other nations and the Ukrainians as well. What support you enjoy from the Russian people derives, for the most part, in their admiration for your love of Mother Russia and its glorious past. But, if they see that this war may negatively impact our standing in the world or them directly, that support will wane. And then, ruling the largest country in the world will become unfeasible."

"I've heard enough," stated Vladimir Putin at long last. "You, Lavrov, and the generals and admirals have all counseled me to cease and desist in my pursuit to bring Ukraine back into the Russian fold. But I have one more group of people I trust with whom I must consult before I make my final decision. The Americans have said that I have until 11:00PM tomorrow evening to give them my response. I plan to use every minute of my remaining time to ensure that I make the correct decision for both the Russian Federation and the Russian people."

Chris Knowles

Chapter Thirty

President Vladimir Putin's final meeting of the day was with a group of men who arguably were nearly as powerful as the president himself and without whose input he seldom made a significant decision. They were the Russian oligarchs. The oligarchy consists of an exclusive cadre of businessmen from the former Soviet republics who used the fall of the Soviet Union and the turbulent period which followed to accumulate great wealth as the Russian economy was undergoing rapid privatization. Emerging from a history during which the state owned or controlled all the means of production, the ownership of state assets was ill-defined and called into question. The oligarchs, most of whom were former government employees and many of whom were previously associated with the KGB, stepped in and purchased previously state-owned properties at rock bottom prices.

Putin and the oligarchs would dine in the sumptuous St. Catherine Hall within the walls of the Grand Kremlin Palace. A room often used for formal and ostentatious award presentations or exclusive conferences, this evening the hall would be outfitted as a dining venue. The most ornate dining tables, finest china, and best silverware would be used as befitted the station in life and status which the oligarchs occupied in 21st century Russia.

Few of the names from within the oligarchy would be well known outside the borders of Russia. They included Roman Abromavich, Mikhail Prokhorov, Viktor Vekselberg, Leonid Mikhelson, and Vitaly Malkin. Among the oligarchs, the group which was rumored to hold the greatest sway with President Putin was known as the *Siloviki*. They were former members of the KGB or other Russian intelligence services who used their knowledge and leverage during the post-Soviet era to gain great power or wealth by trading on the secrets they could either keep or reveal.

Best known among the *Siloviki*, with the exception of Vladimir Putin himself, may be Alexander Lebedev. After graduating from college in 1982, he went to work for the First Chief Directorate of the KGB as a spy. During the 1980s, he lived in London where he was headquartered at the Russian Embassy. He subsequently went to work for Russia's Foreign Intelligence Service until 1992. In each instance, he was under diplomatic cover as an Economic Attaché.

When Lebedev left the employ of the Russian government, he established the Russian Investment-Finance Company. In 1995 that company bought the nearly insolvent National Reserve Bank. However, over time it survived the Russian financial crisis of 1998 to become one of Russia's two largest banks. Its holdings now include 11% of Aeroflot, the Russian national airline, and 44% of Ilyushin Finance Company which owns a significant position within the Russian aircraft-building industry.

As for the dinner that night, Putin had directed the Kremlin head chef to prepare his most notable dishes and to spare no expense. With each course were served the finest wines, most exquisite liqueurs, and most elite brands of vodka. This was no accident. Putin was seeking a warm reception by the oligarchs whom he hoped would support his military adventurism in Ukraine as a precursor to further enriching themselves and their stockholders. After all, the 110 wealthiest individuals in Russia owned 35% of Russia's wealth.

At the conclusion of the dinner, while fresh glasses of vodka were being served all around, Putin rose from his chair at the head of the central table and approached the microphone on the lectern which had been inconspicuously set up at the front of the room during dinner. He lightly tapped the microphone to make sure that it was working and began.

"Good evening, Gentlemen," he said. "It is wonderful to see so many old friends this evening and to meet some new ones for the first time. I invited all of you here tonight to seek your counsel on a matter of eminent importance to both you and the future of Mother Russia. I have a crucial decision to make, and it is not one which I would presume to make without consulting you.

"As you are all aware, eight days ago four contingents of Russian Army troops entered Ukraine and established positions in their three largest cities as well as setting up a command center in central Ukraine. Our Air Force began enforcing a no-fly zone in Ukrainian airspace and we commandeered an airport near the command center from which we could conduct any needed aerial combat operations. We were initially met with nearly no resistance.

"Subsequently, the Ukrainian President, Petro Poroshenko, called U.S. President John Jefferson and requested his help. That help was promised and soon after provided. Aircraft from bases in Italy, Qatar, and initially Turkey, as well as from the deck of an American aircraft carrier in the Black Sea, flew missions over Ukraine to attack both our ground troops and our aircraft at the airport.

"Shortly thereafter I received a phone call from the American president demanding that I withdraw our troops and aircraft. I was convinced then, as I am convinced now, that our armed forces are superior to theirs and that we can successfully occupy Ukraine as a prelude to annexing it as part of the Russian Federation. I did not withdraw either the Army or the Air Force.

"Consequently, the Americans staged another series of attacks. This time they were nominally more successful. There was a significant loss of life to both our soldiers and aircrews. I have now received an ultimatum from President

Jefferson.

"I have been presented with a document outlining the American's demands for our withdrawal and the terms and conditions under which such withdrawal is to take place. A second document enumerates the consequences of not withdrawing. Finally, I have been provided a peace treaty which must be signed, dated, and returned to Washington by 11:00PM Moscow time tomorrow.

"So I come before you tonight to seek your support for our continued campaign to occupy and annex Ukraine. That nation has historically been within the Russian sphere of influence, and I believe that it should be once again. Roughly one-fifth of the residents of Ukraine are ethnic Russians. They would become Russian citizens once again. Finally, our access to Ukraine's warm water ports on the Black Sea would open up markets in the European and African nations which border the Mediterranean.

"Therefore, in conclusion, I seek your endorsement for my agenda before I make my decision, address the nation, and respond to the American's demands. I now open the floor so that you may ask any questions you wish or make any statements you may deem appropriate or necessary."

There were twenty-five men in the room; Vladimir Putin and twenty-four oligarchs. Among the twenty-four, all were millionaires, some tens or hundreds of times over, and a few were billionaires. And they were not like docile school children. They did not raise their hands and wait to be called upon. They all rose from their comfortable chairs, some with drinks still in hand, and began to congregate in groups of four, five, or six against the walls of the opulent hall.

Five, ten, fifteen minutes passed as they continued in rapt conversation. But one man was seen to be circulating among the groups, a few minutes here and a few minutes there. He had silver-gray hair and his ample weight strained against the stitching of his impeccably-tailored Western European suit. He was possessed of piercing eyes and a voice which was hushed and quiet as he was accustomed to engaging in confidential discussions which were not meant to be overheard.

Eventually, the oligarchs returned to their tables and all but one took their seats. The last man standing was Igor Sechin whom every source from London's *Guardian* newspaper to America's CNBC television network have characterized as the second most powerful man in Russia. His widely diversified wealth has been estimated at $1 billion. Putin took note of Sechin standing behind his chair which was just to the right of the one which he himself had occupied throughout their dinner.

Chapter Thirty-one

"Igor Ivanovitch, my old friend," said Putin, using the oligarch's respectful patronymic form of address, "I see you wish to speak. I'm sure that both I and all our assembled friends are anxious to hear what you have to say. Please, please, begin."

The 58-year-old Igor Sechin was Russia's pre-eminent oligarch. Whatever he was about to say would represent the consensus of the twenty-three others in the room. And, when he was done, the burden would fall upon Putin to quell any concerns which the oligarchs had and respond to any demands which they might make.

Like Putin, Sechin had been born in St. Petersburg, only eight years later. And, like Putin, he had been born into a working-class family. He attended Leningrad State University where he earned a PhD in Economics and became fluent in French and Portuguese. He subsequently joined the military and was posted to Angola and Mozambique as a translator. Following his term of military service, he continued in that role as an agent for the KGB.

In 1994, when Vladimir Putin became Deputy Mayor of St. Petersburg, Sechin was hired as his Secretary. He closely protected access to Putin and had a reputation for keeping meticulous notes of all of the Deputy Mayor's meetings. In 1996, when Putin left for Moscow, Sechin followed.

On December 31, 1999, Putin succeeded Boris Yeltsin as President of the Russian Federation. Igor Sechin was named his Deputy Head of Administration overseeing both the security services and energy policies. He also retained his duties as gatekeeper to Putin.

Beginning in 2008, after serving two four-year terms as President, Putin acted as Prime Minister under Dmitry Medvedev for four years. Sechin was named Deputy Premier overseeing, among other things, energy policy. When Putin was re-elected for a six-year term as President in 2012, Sechin became the Chief Executive Officer of Rosneft, the state-controlled oil and natural gas producer.

By now, the role of the oligarchs who came to power in the 1990s had become almost institutionalized. Their wealth and power, as well as their sense of camaraderie and demand for firm state control of the means of production and authoritarian rule, derived, in large part, from their shared former service in the KGB and other state security services. Thus, the *Siloviki* became both influential and feared.

Sechin's association with Putin for a quarter of a century had essentially created a role for him in government service as a *de facto* deputy to the President. Some have pointed out that theirs is a symbiotic relationship wherein each benefits from the influence and strength of the other. Sechin's success at Rosneft, the world's largest publicly listed oil company, provided the Russian state with a significant portion of its annual operating revenue. Therefore, Putin would make no substantive decision without first consulting Sechin.

There were two further aspects to Sechin's persona. The first derived from the fact that Putin was one year into his second six-year term as President. He could not run for a third consecutive term. And there was no heir apparent to the office of President unless Medvedev was willing to accept a second term as nothing more than a placeholder for Putin. In light of the void Putin would leave, there were rumblings that Sechin could be maneuvering for a position as either Prime Minister or President.

The last element to Sechin's reputation was the suspicion and wariness with which he was viewed. A former U.S. ambassador to Moscow characterized Sechin as the "gray cardinal" of the Kremlin "who has sought to break the power of the oligarchs, confiscate and amalgamate their assets into state companies under *Siloviki* control, and to limit Western influence". A 2008 U.S. Embassy cable which was released by Julian Assange's WikiLeaks states that "Sechin was so shadowy that it was joked he may not actually exist but rather was a sort of urban myth, a bogeyman, invented by the Kremlin to instill fear." This, then, would cast him in a role within Russia similar to that of the enigmatic character Keyser Söze in the movie *The Usual Suspects* wherein one character muses about a parent threatening his kid; "Rat on your Pop and Keyser Söze will get you!"

"Thank you, Vladimir," said Sechin in response to Putin's invitation. "We all want to express our gratitude for having been invited here this evening for this excellent meal and fine drink. We also want to thank you for seeking our counsel before any next steps are to be taken in the invasion of our neighboring former republic, Ukraine.

"We want to make sure that we express ourselves clearly and leave no room for misunderstanding." This time Putin took particular note of Sechin's use of the royal "we", denoting that he spoke for not only himself but the other twenty-three men in the room.

"First, we firmly support your domestic policies. Russia is the largest country in the world with widely varying geographies and numerous ethnicities. We endorse your style of authoritarian rule. In a country such as ours, the reins of power must be wielded firmly, lest the people forget who is in charge. We even enjoy your personal style. Being seen fishing or hunting or riding a horse bare-chested gives the common man hope that the values which once characterized the strengths of Mother Russia are not a thing of the past but things which must be pursued and restored.

"But *we* are businessmen. *We* travel the world in corporate jets. *We* cruise the oceans in corporate yachts. But, if truth be told, *we* are always at the mercy of our customers. And most of those customers are in Western countries. Of course, there are always the Chinas and Venezuelas and Cubas. But they are the exception. And we cannot exist on trade with them alone. It is the Western nations on which we made our fortunes; those in Europe and North America.

"In Russia, it is we who *own* the means of production, or *control* the corporations which do, or are the *principal stockholders* who benefit from the increase in the value of their shares. And you have managed to alienate the vast majority of their customers. Most of those nations are members of the European Union, an organization which Ukraine has clearly expressed a desire to join. Most are members of NATO, another organization of which Ukraine has said they want to join.

"When you annexed Crimea five years to the day prior to your invasion of Ukraine, the Western nations imposed trade sanctions on many of the goods and services which our corporations provide. And more recently, when you withdrew from a pact which would enforce a freeze on certain offensive missiles, defensive missiles, and warheads, the West imposed even further trade sanctions on us.

"The only reason we did not come down harder on you five years ago was the fact that the Crimean rebels had broad support from its large ethnic Russian population. But Ukraine is three-quarters ethnic Ukrainians and only one-fifth ethnic Russians. The annexation of Ukraine as part of the Russian Federation will not find favor with our trading partners in the West; those which we have not already lost.

"When we lose customers, demand for our output goes down. When demand for our output goes down, the need for Russian labor decreases. And when employment in the towns where our facilities are located goes down, crime and civil unrest increases. You know your history, Vladimir. The last time Russia experienced widespread civil unrest, the Bolsheviks stormed the Winter Palace, the Winter residence of the Czars, in our hometown.

"Now I'm not saying that the man on the street is anywhere near storming your residence in the Kremlin. But I am saying that your continued military adventurism is going to continue to erode our customer base and that your continued antagonism of the NATO nations could well bring about an unanticipated response.

"As I said at the beginning," Sechin said in conclusion, "*we* are businessmen. When we lose customers, we lose business. And when nations impose trade sanctions, we lose customers. This has to stop *now*. If you want our support for the next five years, this *will* stop *now*!"

Chapter Thirty-two

At the conclusion of the banquet with the oligarchs, Vladimir Putin returned to his residence in the Kremlin. He slowly made his way to the den. With the lights still turned off, he walked across the room to the wet bar and poured himself a snifter of brandy. Then he shuffled over and sat down in the rich, overstuffed red leather chair in front of the now-blazing fire in the fireplace which had been ignited before his arrival by the residence staff.

This was not the first time he had been dressed down by the oligarchs in his now fifteen years as Russia's president. Nor would it be the last. They needed him to be responsive to their policy demands in order to maximize their corporations' profits and their own personal wealth. But he needed their backing in order to govern Russia.

He swirled the brandy around in the snifter, held it up and looked through it at the firelight, and then took a healthy gulp. Had he done all of this for the future glory of Mother Russia or solely to feed his own ego? He both valued and resented the influence of the oligarchs. He valued that their support made it far easier to govern than it would have been without, but he resented the fact that their agendas frequently took the form of demands as related to economic or foreign policy.

In the end, he came to the realization that he would be impotent to continue to prosecute the war in Ukraine without the consent of the oligarchs and the large segment of the Russian population which depended upon their corporations for the income which allowed them to support themselves and their families. He concluded that the only realistic course of action would be to capitulate to President Jefferson's demands. He had four brief phone calls he had to make before the brandy and sleep overtook him.

The first would be to Dmitry Medvedev, the Prime Minister. The second would be to Foreign Minister Lavrov. The third would go to General Sergeyev and the fourth to the network headquarters of Rossiya 1, the state-owned television network based in Moscow. The network had a small, permanent studio in the Kremlin from which announcements by government officials were frequently broadcast. He put them on notice that he would address the Russian nation at Noon on Friday.

The next morning, Putin followed his usual routine of dressing, eating breakfast as he scanned the headlines from the world's leading newspapers, and going to his private office. This morning, he would spend his time writing and re-writing his address to the nation. In the end, his speech was somewhat anticlimactic. It was nothing more than a statement that, in the beginning, he believed that the annexation of Ukraine was in the best interests of both the Ukrainians and the Russian people. But, in the end, he had come to the conclusion that the Ukrainians valued their sovereignty more than the security of becoming a vital part of the Russian Federation.

At the end of the transmission, Putin returned to his office. He sought out and received the assistance of one of his tech-savvy staff members who demonstrated to him how to digitally sign and date the peace treaty which had been transmitted to Foreign Minister Lavrov two days earlier. When the executed document had been completed and saved, the file was transmitted over a secure network connection to Lavrov's office.

The previous evening, Putin had instructed Lavrov that, when he received the signed treaty, he was to transmit it to U.S. Secretary of State Wainwright with no further comment or communication. He did as he was told. The document arrived in Secretary Wainwright's inbox at 5:30AM Washington time Friday morning. The watch officer who monitored the Secretary's incoming transmissions called Wainwright at home and informed him of the arrival of the executed document.

Wainwright, in turn, called the White House switchboard and instructed the operator to put him through to President Jefferson's private phone line in the residence. In truth, Jefferson had been awake since 4:00AM awaiting the receipt of the executed peace treaty, having monitored Russian state TV for the 40 hours since presenting

Ambassador Antonov with the document, when Putin made his address to his people. Jefferson and Wainwright exchanged mutually-congratulatory expressions of joy and relief. Jefferson then directed Wainwright to have the treaty transmitted to President Poroshenko's office in Kiev.

President Jefferson then got on the line to Poroshenko in Vinnytsia. The Ukrainian President was already aware of Putin's "surrender" as he had been watching Rossiya 1 and was expecting Jefferson's call. The President told Poroshenko it was now safe to return to Kiev and that once he was back in his office there would be a peace treaty awaiting him which needed to be signed, dated, and returned to Secretary Wainwright as an attachment to an email.

Poroshenko thanked President Jefferson profusely for the United States' intervention in the conflict. He also expressed his profound regret for the loss of the American airmen's lives and assured him that their remains would be returned to the United States as soon as possible as would the surviving pilots who had been taken in by grateful Ukrainians during the conflict.

Jefferson modestly accepted Poroshenko's thanks and told him that an American transport would fly into Kiev within the next twenty-four hours to pick up both the surviving airmen as well as the remains of those killed in combat. Poroshenko assured Jefferson that all would be in order when the American aircraft arrived. He thanked

Jefferson yet again and then prepared to return to Kiev for the signing of the treaty.

Over the next hour, the White House Press Office prepared a statement announcing that President Putin had signed a treaty ending the hostilities on the ground and in the air above Ukraine. It was released as quickly as possible so that it could be the lead story on *The Today Show*, *Good Morning America*, *CBS This Morning*, and *Fox & Friends*.

At Aviano Air Base in Italy, one of the C-17 *Globemaster IIIs* which had been shuttling between California and Italy carrying the BLU-129/Bs was put on call. On Saturday after sundown, it was to land in Kiev to pick up the surviving pilots as well as the remains of the deceased airmen. From there it would fly to Ramstein Air Base in Germany. Both the airmen and the remains would be transported to Landstuhl Regional Medical Center where the survivors would undergo extensive screenings, both physical and mental, while the remains would be prepared for their repatriation when they arrived on American soil.

Later Friday morning, President Jefferson huddled with Secretary of State Wainwright and National Security Advisor Winstead in the Oval Office. While the subject of their conversation may have seemed trivial to outsiders, it bore heavily upon both diplomatic relations and military confrontations. The question on the table was whether or not President Jefferson would address the nation on live TV, as Putin had done only hours earlier, to announce the cessation of hostilities with the Russians over Ukrainian autonomy or to simply grant a series of interviews with Secretary Wainwright to the major networks to discuss the prosecution and culmination of the conflict with Russia.

A live TV address would give an event which should never have happened the same status as 9/11 or the capture and death of bin Laden. Regrettably, such an address would give Russia's allies, as well as other third parties, fodder to further stoke the flames of retaliation and terrorism against the West. In the end, all three agreed that interviews with Secretary Wainwright were the way to go.

The once "blood and guts" Joint Chiefs' Chairman had evolved into an even-tempered and subdued Secretary of State who could handle even the most contentious of journalists who were trying to get a rise out of him. In doing so, the interview ultimately concluded without giving the interviewer any morsel of controversy or vindictiveness upon which to construct a false or misleading narrative.

Vladimir Putin had swallowed his pride while currying still greater favor with the oligarchs who possessed the power to make or break him. He had five years to go in his fourth term as President of the Russian Federation. They could be easy or they could be hard. Fomenting world war could never end well while preserving the status quo kept everyone happy. Especially the businessmen.

Epilogue

At precisely Noon on Tuesday, March 12th, the Air Force C-17 *Globemaster III* touched down at Dover Air Force Base, Delaware. It slowed and taxied to a hangar whose door was raised and which was festooned with red, white, and blue bunting. Once it had come to a full stop, it lowered its large aft ramp.

A contingent of both civilian and military dignitaries was assembled just outside the hangar led by President John Jefferson and Secretary of State Charles Wainwright, accompanied by the Secretary of Defense and the Chairman of the Joint Chiefs of Staff. Six caskets were carried down the ramp by Navy honor guards and taken to six ebony-black biers located just inside the hangar door. They were followed by the surviving pilots who had been sheltered by the Ukrainians after their aircraft had been shot out from beneath them. Starting with the President, each of the dignitaries walked by the six caskets, everyone stopping at each of the caskets to pay their respects. Next, they walked over to the pilots, either shaking hands with or saluting each of them.

The President then walked over to a podium set up just behind the caskets while the remainder of those in attendance re-assembled at the hangar's entrance. His comments were brief. He paid respects to the deceased while acknowledging the contribution of both the living aviators and the dead to world peace. Afterward, both he and the Secretary of State re-boarded Marine One for the helicopter ride back to the South Lawn of the White House. The entire ceremony had been televised nationwide on live TV by all four major networks.

* * *

On Friday, March 31st, the Ukrainian people went to the polls to cast their votes for President. The two candidates who garnered the greatest number of votes were incumbent President Petro Poroshenko, a man of inexhaustible political ambition, and actor and comedian Volodymyr Zelensky. Poroshenko, the virulently anti-Russian candidate, received 16% of the vote while Zelensky received 30%. They would next run against one another in the second round of voting on Sunday, April 21st.

In that second round, Zelensky received 73.22%, or nearly three-quarters, of the vote while Poroshenko could only attract 24.45%, less than one-quarter. Thus, there would be a change in regimes in Ukraine, one upon which Jefferson and his advisors had not counted. The new president, a 41-year-old political newcomer, would take office on Thursday, May 30th.

While Zelensky had no track record which the American administration could use to evaluate or anticipate the policies and positions which the new president would adopt or take, the anxiety which had gripped many heads of state at the prospect of an actor taking on the role of politician was not necessarily called for. There were, after all, precedents for actors becoming successful politicians. Two notable examples existed in America alone.

The lesser was Clint Eastwood. In April of 1986, at the age of 55, Eastwood ran for and won the nonpartisan position of Mayor of the town of Carmel-by-the-Sea in California. Subsequently, Democrat Governor Gray Davis appointed him to the California State Park and Recreation Commission.

But Eastwood's most infamous political endeavor did not occur until 2012. That year he endorsed Republican presidential candidate Mitt Romney. He was invited to address the Republican National Convention in Tampa, Florida.

On the evening of Thursday, August 30th, the night on which Romney would accept his party's nomination for President, Eastwood made a surprise appearance in the final hour of the nationally-broadcast convention. When he took the stage there was an empty chair placed nearby the podium facing Eastwood where he was meant to stand to speak. The bulk of his appearance consisted of what was clearly intended to be an interview of the incumbent Democrat President. The first impression was that interviewing him was comparable to interviewing an "empty suit". Eastwood's "interview" was both viscerally aggressive and unapologetically piercing. Although his performance met with mixed reviews from around the world of entertainment, it was an unqualified success with the convention's delegates.

Without any need for discussion, the single greatest accomplishment of an actor transforming himself into a politician can be found in the life and legacy of Ronald Reagan. Already an actor before World War II, Reagan was commissioned a second lieutenant in the Officers' Reserve Corps of the Cavalry on May 25th, 1937. At the conclusion of the war, he was separated from active duty on December 9th, 1945.

Reagan's first foray into politics was with the Screen Actors Guild (SAG). He first became President of SAG in 1947. He was ultimately elected to seven one-year terms from 1947 until 1952 and again in 1959. He marshaled the union through the turbulent years of the House Un-American Activities Committee hearings and Hollywood's "Blacklist" era.

Ronald Reagan was strongly anti-Communist and said, "I never as a citizen want to see our country become urged, by either fear or resentment of this group, that we ever compromise with any of our democratic principles through that fear or resentment." Although a lifelong

Democrat, he changed party affiliation to Republican in 1962 and became a leading conservative spokesman for the Barry Goldwater campaign in 1964. He was often quoted as saying, "I didn't leave the Democratic Party. The party left me."

In 1965, Reagan announced the formation of a campaign committee to manage his run for election as the next Governor of California in November of 1966. His campaign focused on two main issues. The first was, in his terms, "to send the welfare bums back to work." The second, motivated by the violent anti-Vietnam War protests which were tearing the main campus of The University of California apart, was "to clean up the mess at Berkeley." He defeated two-term Governor Pat Brown and was sworn in on January 2nd, 1967. He was re-elected to a second term in 1970.

In 1976, Reagan sought the Republican presidential nomination over incumbent Gerald Ford but failed in his bid. Four years later, Reagan sought and won the Republican presidential nomination and the right to run against then-incumbent Democrat President Jimmy Carter. The two candidates could not have been more politically at odds. At the core of the contest was the simple fact that Carter, although a graduate of Annapolis and a former nuclear submarine Executive Officer, was a "dove" while Reagan, the outspoken anti-Communist, was a "hawk". Throughout the campaign, the specter of the Iran hostage crisis in which 52 American diplomats and citizens had been captured at the American Embassy in Tehran and were being held hostage by Muslim rebels as part of the Iranian Revolution hung over the proceedings.

On November 4th, 1980, Ronald Reagan defeated Jimmy Carter for the presidency. On January 20th, 1981, after 444 days in captivity, the 52 American hostages in Iran were released and exited Iranian airspace just as newly-inaugurated President Ronald Reagan completed his twenty-minute inaugural address. The two most notable characteristics of the eight-year Reagan Era were the stabilization and re-growth of the American economy which had suffered under the influence of "stagflation" under President Jimmy Carter and the revitalization of America's military might.

The Soviet Union had undergone a financial collapse in the mid-1980s. Whatever benefits those nations within their sphere of influence had enjoyed for the past 35+ years had been dissipated. The period of economic stagnation and lack of financial incentive to stay within the Soviet fold had led to a state where the impetus to support the Soviet model had crumbled.

Ultimately, in the denouement of the collapse of the hegemony of the Soviet Union over Eastern Europe, President Reagan traveled to Berlin in the Summer of 1987. The President and his wife were taken to the Reichstag where they viewed the Berlin Wall from the balcony. At 2:00PM on the afternoon of June 12th, Reagan gave a speech at the Brandenburg Gate behind two panes of bulletproof glass. In the audience were West German President Richard von Weizsäcker, Chancellor Helmut Kohl, and West Berlin Mayor Eberhard Diepgen.

Reagan looked out at both the dignitaries and the assembled crowd and began.

"We welcome change and openness; for we believe that freedom and security go together, that the advance of human liberty can only strengthen the cause of world peace. There is one sign the Soviets can make that would be unmistakable, that would advance dramatically the cause of freedom and peace. General Secretary Gorbachev, if you seek peace, if you seek prosperity for the Soviet Union and Eastern Europe, if you seek liberalization, come here to this gate. Mr. Gorbachev, open this gate. Mr. Gorbachev . . . Mr. Gorbachev, tear down this wall!"

With those five simple sentences, President Ronald Reagan changed the course of future diplomatic relations between the East and West and world history. Shortly before a press conference which was scheduled for November 9th, Gunter Schabowski, an East Berlin party boss, was charged with the duty of announcing new regulations regarding the Berlin Wall. Unfortunately, he had neither been involved in the discussions regarding the wall nor been fully updated.

Shortly before his press conference, he was handed a note outlining the changes in regulations regarding the wall but had been given no instructions as to how to handle the information. The new regulations were to have taken effect the next day so as to allow time for the border guards to be informed of them, but he had been given no information to that effect. At the culmination of his press conference, Schabowski read aloud the note he had been given. When a reporter asked when the new regulations were to take effect, Schabowski said, "As far as I know, it takes effect immediately, without delay." Upon further questioning by journalists, he confirmed that the regulations included the border crossings through the Wall into West Berlin, which he had not mentioned until then.

Later that night on national television, anchorman Hanns Joachin Friedrichs stated, "This 9 November is a historic day. The GDR (Democratic Republic of Germany) has announced that starting immediately, its borders are open to everyone. The gates in the Wall stand open wide." It was the culminating and signature moment of the Reagan presidency.

Following the broadcast, East Germans began gathering at the Wall, at the six checkpoints between East and West Berlin, demanding that border guards immediately open the gates. It soon became clear that no one among the East German authorities would take personal responsibility so the soldiers had no way to hold back the huge crowd of East German citizens. Finally, at 10:45PM, the commander of the border crossing yielded, allowing the guards to open the checkpoints and permitting people through without vetting. As the Easterners rushed through the gates, they were greeted by Westerners waiting with flowers and champagne. Soon, a crowd of West Berliners mounted the Wall and were shortly thereafter joined by East Germans. The fall of the Berlin Wall began on the evening of the 9th of November, 1989. It continued over the following days and weeks with people using whatever they could get their hands on to chip off souvenirs, destroying lengthy segments in the process and creating unofficial border crossings.

With one sentence, President Reagan had changed the face of Europe forever and, in the process, given hope to a whole new generation of free men. Could new Ukrainian President Zelensky hope to cultivate a following and leave a legacy which would endear him to a new generation of Ukrainians for decades to come? There was no way to know. But the opportunity existed. The door to a new Ukraine stood before him. All he needed was confidence in himself and faith in the Ukrainian people to lead them into the European Union, the North Atlantic Treaty Organization, and the 21st century.

The End

Made in the USA
Middletown, DE
03 November 2022

14054734R00154